W9-AWK-472

# The Exchange Student

# the exchange student

kate gilmore

Houghton Mifflin Company
Boston

For Jack



The text of this book is set in eleven-point Slimbach.

*Library of Congress Cataloging-in-Publication Data*

Gilmore, Kate.
The exchange student / Kate Gilmore.
p. cm.
Summary: When her mother arranges to host one of the young people coming to Earth from Chela, Daria is both pleased and intrigued by the keen interest shown by the Chelan in her work breeding endangered species.
ISBN 0-395-57511-7
[1. Wildlife conservation—Fiction. 2. Endangered species—Fiction. 3. Extraterrestrials—Fiction.] I. Title.
PZ7.G4374Ex 1999
[Fic]—dc21 97-47162 CIP AC

Printed in the United States of America

**QUM 10 9 8 7 6 5**

## acknowledgments

I am enormously grateful to all the busy people who were so patient with my questions about animals.

Alan Sironen, curator of mammals at the Cleveland Metro Park Zoo, spent the morning talking with me and searching his library for articles about binturongs. He also, to my immeasurable delight, allowed me to pet the binturongs in his care and to watch them after closing time when they are at their liveliest. Jeff Munson, that large keeper of tiny animals at the Bronx Zoo, was always ready to pause in his hectic routine to discuss anything from dwarf mongooses to space travel. Thanks also to Kim Tropea for long talks over the monkey chow in the kitchen of the small primate house and to Kitty Dolan, senior keeper of the Bronx Zoo's Jungle World, who shared her binturong lore with me on numerous occasions. Steve Cepregi of the Philadelphia Zoo was a mine of information about fennec foxes and many other fascinating creatures. My old friend Alexander Goldowsky of the New England Aquarium showed me enough wonders in an afternoon to fill yet another book.

We owe a special debt to Diane Ackerman for writing *The Moon By Whale Light*, a book which changed my casual love of animals to something altogether more profound.

Warm thanks are also due to my readers—to Valerie and Geoff and Kay and Than and, of course, to Jack, who had the big idea that made the book so much harder to write and so much more interesting.

# prologue

"So why send a gaggle of kids? I mean, it's almost insulting, right? We send five expeditions of the best and the brightest—astronauts first, of course, then all kinds of scientists, anthropologists, even an art historian this last time around. Everybody's waiting to see what Chela will send to us, and what do they send? Kids."

"I've heard they respect their young people more than we do ours," said another voice, "and that these are pretty special kids—special in what way I couldn't tell you."

"And I say who cares?" a third voice said. "So long as they get them off that ship and into our welcoming arms. My kid goes to Shanghai, and we've got a rocket to catch."

The nine escorts from the Terran-Chelan Cultural Exchange Bureau stared through the cold fog at the sleek form of the transfer module that stood across the runway and stubbornly refused to disgorge its passengers. The year was 2094, the historic occasion the arrival of the first ship from the planet Chela, bringing nine adolescent Chelans to live with carefully chosen families on Earth. They had been sent with the understanding that no fanfare was to attend their arrival. They were to melt into their widely scattered habitats like snow, or so the improbable theory went.

At last the door to the module slid back, and the exchange students came down the stairs and gathered at the far end of their ship. It was hard to see, for the visitors were as grey as the mist and largely unclothed, their silvery skin shimmering faintly against the dark runway. "What are they doing?" whispered Penny Mackleby. She was the youngest of the escorts and the most afraid. She had a sign pinned to her coat with WELCOME FEN printed in big red letters.

The tall, fragile figures had formed a circle on the black tarmac of the spaceport and seemed to perform some ceremony of farewell as each reached out to touch the amulet that hung around the neck of the one across from him. For a long moment they were still, their heads bowed, their dark hair blowing in the wind.

Then suddenly the circle broke, and the young Chelans came bounding across the tarmac, waving and calling out their names. The escorts formed a line and stood their ground, pointing to their signs and calling out in turn the names of the exchange students who had been assigned to them. After a brief skirmish, all were paired off—all except Penny and Fen. Fen at the last second had veered away and now could be seen on his knees by the entrance to the terminal where someone had tied a tiny mongrel dog.

"Fen, don't!" Penny cried. All she needed was to have her charge bitten in his first five minutes on Earth.

He seemed not to hear. He knelt, his long limbs folded like a grasshopper's legs, in an attitude almost of prayer before the scruffy little animal, and Penny saw that he was not going to be bitten. Slowly the dog's tail stirred the dust, its ears came forward, and finally its pink tongue lapped the thin grey fingers of the alien.

# one

Daria woke early and without help from her computer, which was given to reminding her of things she would have preferred to forget. She woke because most of the forty-five animals that occupied various cages and enclosures around the edges of her room were early risers and were yelling for their breakfasts. A crash from the binturongs' cage announced that they had knocked over the boxes piled up for their entertainment the night before.

"Hell," Daria said. "Scorpions and rattlesnakes." Up on one elbow now, she peered from the edge of her loft bed at the surrounding zoo. Aside from the boxes, all seemed to be well. And the boxes were no problem either—just noisy. The binturongs had had their game and, being nocturnal, would soon be sacked out like a pair of shaggy throw rugs in their nest. Directly across from Daria's bed, in one of the two big plastic bubbles that bulged out from the end of her room, the hornbills were calling the dwarf mongooses to come out of their cozy burrows and help hunt crickets through the grass. One problem there: no crickets. And no marmoset chow for the tamarins, no fruit for the mynas, no mice for the green tree boa, no meat for the foxes, to mention only a few items that were not only missing but also not even prepared.

Daria moaned and sank back on her pillow. She always fixed the animals' breakfast the night before. Always. It was an ironclad rule designed to avoid exactly the prospect that now confronted her, namely an hour and a half in the kitchen slicing carrots, chopping kale, opening food packs, thawing mice, and sprinkling supplements. At dawn, when one was not at one's most efficient.

Remembering the reason for this lapse, Daria sat bolt upright, grabbed the rumpled tunic she had shoved into the crack between bed and wall, and scrambled down the ladder. Last night her mother, the famous and beautiful, if not always too bright, Gloria Wells, had made an announcement to her assembled family. "I have a lovely surprise for you," Gloria had said, smiling bravely at the row of four dubious faces. "An exchange student from the planet Chela is coming to live with us, starting tomorrow. Sorry not to give you more warning, darlings, but I know you'll cope. It should be a wonderful experience for all of us." The discussion, if that is the right word, that followed these remarks had kept Daria up long past her usual bedtime and drained her of the will to chop even the smallest leaf of kale.

She tore down the hall barefoot, her disgraceful tunic flapping around her thighs, and into the kitchen, where she paused to catch her breath. It was now 6:30, and the exchange student was due at 9:00—enough time to fix the animals' food, distribute it, and check everyone out; not by any means enough time to get used to the idea that a teenage male humanoid from space was about to take up residence in the spare room. What does he eat? Daria wondered, dragging a sack of carrots out of the mammoth refrigerator her father had bought when the zoo first showed signs of expanding beyond the frog-and-baby-robin stage. When does he sleep? How does he vocalize? She realized that she was thinking, as usual, like a zoologist. A normal person would be wondering whether the visitor would be nice, fun to be with, easy to talk to, hopelessly weird, or just sort of different. "Very tall, very thin, pale grey in color," Daria said to the large bunch of kale that had joined the carrots on the chopping board.

A voice behind her made her jump. "How about hollow bones, large brains, rapid metabolism," the voice said, and Daria turned to smile at her father. She saw that he was dressed for work in a straight, dark green tunic and narrow charcoal trousers. This observation was not a happy one, for it suggested that her father, a rather exalted landscape architect and city planner who could work when he pleased, was about to abandon ship.

"You're not thinking of leaving before the exchange student comes?" Daria said, without much hope.

The expressive dark face registered fathoms of regret. "I'd give anything to be here when this fellow arrives, but duty calls. Somebody, after all, must support this less than minimal establishment." He waved at the gleaming kitchen and the spacious grounds that could be seen through its long windows. "I have an enormously important appointment that would be worth my whole career to skip."

"You lie," Daria said amiably, dumping portions of variously cut vegetables into the labeled metal bowls.

"Will he like animals, I wonder?" said Roger Wells.

"It would be nice," Daria said wistfully. "It would be a really pleasant change from the rest of this household."

"Present company excepted, of course."

Daria smiled. "Present company is always excepted." She sprinkled a tray of wriggling mealworms with calcium powder.

Her father craned his neck. "Yum. What's that? Worms with powdered sugar? You're spoiling those critters."

"Calcium, as you perfectly well know," Daria said. "The powder sticks to the worms, but better yet, they eat it, so by tonight I'll have a whole tray of calcium-loaded goodies to hand out."

"Diabolical."

"Isn't it?"

"How are the binturongs?" Roger asked. "Any sign of a blessed event?"

"You can't tell a thing with all that fur," Daria said. "She doesn't look any different pregnant than she did before, but fortunately there's no mystery about the gestation period. She's due in about a week. You can order my straitjacket now."

"A lot of good you'll be to your birthing mother in a straitjacket," Roger said. "Is it really that nerve-racking? You've had lots of baby animals born since you got your license to breed endangered species, including, as I recall, some fairly tricky ones."

"She's very young, and she might have quads. It runs in her family, and it's a worry for me because the fourth one often doesn't survive. Also young binturong mothers sometimes don't care for their babies, but you're not supposed to interfere or jump to conclusions. If you go into the cage too soon, you can cause just what you're trying to prevent. If you don't go in, one or more may die of neglect. It's not the kind of thing that makes someone as new as I am to the breeding program exactly relaxed."

"What does Giovanna say?"

"Giovanna says, '*Cara mia,* do not worry so much. They're not that rare.' But you know what an uproar there was at the Ark when she decided I could have the binturongs to breed. I mean, it's not like they were the last ones on Earth, but still, if I lose a baby, I'll cut my throat."

"If you lose a baby, it will probably be due to something you could neither have foreseen nor prevented," Roger said. "Giovanna's right. You worry too much. I suppose you're overworked."

"Who, me? Whatever would give you that idea?"

"And now you'll have a creature from space to look after."

Daria put down her knife and stared at her father. "Very funny," she said. "But seriously, Dad, what do you think? Has Mom gone completely round the bend? I mean, what is all this 'Sorry I never got around to mentioning it, but we're about to have a semipermanent alien in the house'?"

"Your mother is an exceptionally warm, impulsive woman."

"Impulsive, my foot. She applied to this exchange thing six months ago."

"She's also something of a coward," Roger admitted.

"Who's a coward?" Lily, in a creamy floor-length tunic and gold sandals, stood in the doorway to the kitchen. Like her mother, she was as fair as Roger and Daria were dark—glamorous, beautiful, and, in her younger sister's opinion, a class-A bitch. "Mom, I suppose," Lily answered herself, and drifted a few feet into the kitchen. "What else is new? God, Daria, aren't you supposed to do that stuff at night? I want my breakfast."

"So have your breakfast," Daria said, pointing to the food slots along the far wall of the kitchen. "Nothing's stopping you. Just let me get the mice out of the fridge, and you can have the counter." She moved the mealworms, which should have been put on a shelf for the night feeding, a little more center stage.

"Disgusting," Lily said, "and that means you and your creepy animals and their revolting food. Daddy, for the ninety-ninth time, when can I go away to school?"

"You don't want to stick around for the exchange student?" Roger asked disingenuously, since the topic had been well covered the night before. The answer was no.

"The exchange student is the final straw. Talk about creepy." Lily began to edge along the wall toward the food slots, keeping as far away as possible from the animal food.

"How do you know he's creepy?" Daria asked. "I think the Chelans look quite distinguished in their pictures. You may fall madly in love and go off to Chela to design bath sarongs. That seems to be about all they wear."

Lily, who was in fact an aspiring clothes designer, gave her sister a venomous look. "They're grey," she said, as if that settled the matter. "And what would you know about creepy? Anyone who gets off on bats and snakes is warped from birth."

Roger Wells sighed. He was fond of both of his daughters and wished they would be more tolerant of each other. Wrangling, however, was not his cup of tea and usually brought on a disappearing act. "Well, girls, I must be off into the great world," he said, the door to the garden already half-open, one foot on the threshold of freedom.

"Daddy, don't go," Lily wailed, but her father blew a kiss and was gone. "Now look what you've done." She gave one of the buttons that lined the wall a savage jab and produced a box of diet cereal. A carton of skim milk plopped out of the next slot, and Lily began edging back toward the hall.

"Who, me?" Daria said. "We were doing fine until you arrived. Oh, lovely. Here comes Tim. He seems to have done something new to his hair."

The third Wells sibling regarded his sisters with slightly

bleary good nature from the hallway door. He was a good-looking boy, or might have been but for his recent fascination with the culture of the 1970s. He was olive-skinned and blue-eyed. About his hair it was hard to say. Currently it was lavender and projected from his head in artfully contrived spikes.

"You look like a freak," Lily pronounced, and her twin grinned happily.

"I'm freaked out," Tim said. His misuse of this archaic phrase was lost on Lily and Daria. For all they knew, it was an exact description of the drooping figure in the doorway. "Get me some coffee, Lil. Be a love and save a life."

"Get it yourself," Lily snapped. "Can't you see my hands are full?"

Tim sighed and drifted over to the coffee slot, wrinkling his nose at the animal food as he went by. "Aren't you supposed to do that stuff at night?"

"The next person to say that is going to get a face full of mealworms," Daria said.

"Oh, sorry. No offense, old thing."

"In case it has slipped your mind," she continued, "we were up quite late last night having what passes for a discussion in this family."

"How could I forget?" Tim said. "That's actually why I'm up at this awful hour. The barbarian must be virtually at the gates. What time is it?"

Lily looked at her watch. "Seven-fifteen, you hopeless twerp. You could have slept another hour at least."

Tim groaned. "It's my damn computer. It delights in

practical jokes at my expense. Where's Dad? Since I'm up anyway, maybe I can get another amplifier out of him while he's still sleepy."

"If you were ever up early, you would know that Dad is at his absolutely most alert and wary just shortly after dawn," Daria said. "But you're saved from making a horrid mistake. He ducked out ten minutes ago. Also, you don't want another amplifier, Tim. You really don't."

"I do."

"Do you want everyone else in the house to move out?" Lily inquired unwisely.

"Do you think one more amp will do it?"

"I wonder if the alien will have sensitive ears," Daria said. "Oh Lord, I wonder a lot of things, but soon we'll know. Does anyone but me feel just the faintest shiver up the spine?"

"I thought weirdness was your thing," Lily said, "like the more bizarre the better."

"Animals can be very strange," Daria said slowly. "They live in another world. They can be mysterious and totally surprising. There's so much I don't know, so much nobody knows. Still, the strangest animal on Earth can be related to some other animal or to some evolutionary principle. But an alien is something else—really something else. That's what the word means, doesn't it? Alien. Not just strange but unknowable—a sort of black hole in your head."

Lily yawned. "I wasn't really asking for a philosophy lecture," she said, and Daria slammed the cleaver into the chunk of meat she was cutting up for the foxes. Her sister got the point and headed for the garden door with her cereal and milk clutched to her chest. “Breakfast by the pond, I think,” said Lily.

“Watch out for the geese,” Daria said. “They haven’t been fed.”

“I’ll strangle the first goose that goes for my cereal.”

“Lots of luck,” said Daria. The geese were large, tame, and extremely aggressive.

Lily kicked open the kitchen door and disappeared into the garden. Daria and Tim maintained a hopeful silence, soon rewarded by a shriek of rage, indignant honking, and the bang of another door as their sister retreated into the front of the house.

“She knows better,” Tim commented.

“If she’d just take some dry bread.”

“It takes a lot of bread to stave off those beasts. This coffee is ghastly.”

“Mom said we could get a real coffeepot if we’d brew it ourselves and clean up afterward.” Daria pulled a trolley with three long shelves from under the counter and began to stack it with bowls and trays. “Speaking of Mom, I wonder where she is on this day of days.”

“Tidying the house with Esfor,” Tim said. “I saw them hard at it in the living room—Mom giving orders in all the wrong sequences, Esfor sitting in the middle of the rug buzzing helplessly.”

Daria laughed. Esfor—its name a simple derivation of its serial number—was their rather primitive household robot. Roger Wells, who could have afforded a more sophisticated model, felt that doing some of the housework put his family in touch with reality. "I wonder if our visitor cares for tidiness," she said. "Perhaps he's just another messy teenager."

"He probably likes beer and chippos and good, loud wallow."

"You hope."

"Of course I do. It'd be a relief from all this earnestness."

"Meaning me."

"Meaning you and meaning my lovely twin sister, who may be talented but whose designs lack the faintest trace of humor."

"Well, sorry to be a bore," Daria said. "There's something about four dozen hungry mouths to feed that puts a damper on frivolity. See you later, Tim. Try not to sleep through the great event."

"No chance. I actually drank this awful brew, and now I'm wide-awake."

"In that case, maybe you could feed the llamas and the outdoor birds. I'm hideously behind."

"I'm not that wide-awake," Tim said, moving purposefully toward the hall. "The term was relative, dear Sis."

"Why did I ask?" Daria gave the trolley an angry shove, and Tim jumped out of her way.

# two

Fen gazed through the window of the monorail as it slid over the flooded delta of the Housatonic River in southern Connecticut. Tall wading birds stood in the dazzling sheet of water watching for a fishy breakfast. White gulls wheeled overhead. Fen rehearsed the names of the birds in his mind—crested kingfisher, great egret, herring gull. A herring was a fish, so the gulls were fishing, too, but in a different way. He sighed happily and glanced over at the young Earth woman in the seat next to him. Penny slept in an awkward position with her head twisted to one side. She would have a stiff neck, and Fen was tempted to waken her. He was deterred by the fact that Penny, even at the cost of a stiff neck, preferred to sleep. She was cross when awakened every hour, as Fen had discovered during the course of the night.

He, too, required frequent naps and even more frequent meals, but for his particular biology a long nocturnal train ride was ideal. He had dozed and wakened, munched and stared. The evening was long in this northern spring, and Fen's eyes were well adapted to the dusk. As the train slowed just before total darkness, he had seen a wave of bats emerge from a wooded hillside and disperse in dizzying spirals against the darkening sky. After dark he had peered out at the towns and villages of rural Maine. There were hamlets lighted by only a few soft lamps through which the train slipped without pause, larger towns where it made brief stops against almost deserted platforms, and at last, near dawn, the glittering towers of Boston rising behind their dikes. It was fascinating. It was too much. Even in the dark Fen felt his senses overload. "Why?" he had cried. "What? Who? Where? When?" And Penny, who with each passing hour more bitterly regretted her decision to take the train, had tried to answer him.

Had his companion not been so increasingly grouchy, the hours since boarding the train at the Canadian spaceport would have been perfect bliss, for they had been occupied by seeing new sights, asking questions, napping, and eating. What more could any Chelan ask?

Fen smiled at the thought of all the edible delights that the train had offered and that Penny had brought, at first gladly, but with less enthusiasm as the night wore on, to their compartment—carnivorous delights called hamburgers and hot dogs, crunchy things, sweet round things with holes in the middle. The meat, Penny had said, was real meat—something Fen had never had. Turning his unusually flexible mind away from the thought that where there was meat, there were dead animals, he spent a few moments contemplating the great variety of new foods that lay ahead, for Chelans were omnivorous in the extreme and seldom turned up their beaky grey noses at anything that could be munched, crunched, or slurped.

He decided to let Penny sleep, even though a major question had come to mind as he looked out over the beautiful but unpopulated wetlands. Had this part of the Connecticut coast been abandoned when, seventy-five years ago, the seas of the planet had begun their dramatic and catastrophic rise? The dikes of Boston had been no surprise to Fen. His own planet was diked from stem to stern and had been for centuries. He supposed the Terrans had been in a hurry—had had to pick and choose—which must have been hard on the people who had lived on this coast. Still, it made a wonderful aquatic habitat, and Fen, who cared less for people than for animals, was grateful for that.

Beyond the river delta the train came into a landscape of low hills and stopped at another small town. Fen flattened his nose against the glass. He was baffled and charmed by the great diversity of housing on Earth and had not been able to get a satisfactory explanation from Penny, who seemed to feel that a desire for variety in dwelling places was completely normal. Fen shrugged. Perhaps it was. In the dark ages of his own planet, the Chelans, too, had built homes without a trace of uniformity. There had been mud huts and castles, hivelike structures holding many families, and isolated houses. But all this had been very long ago, in a period of Chelan history everyone preferred not to think about.

Here the houses were more various than any Fen had seen so far. Some were very large, with solar panels opening like great dark wings on top. Each house had its own windmill, often of a fanciful design, and each was surrounded by broad-leaved trees. Soon, he understood, it would grow very warm, and then, during the broiling heat of summer, school would begin in the vast, cool underground chambers that had been built for this purpose after the environmental crash of the twenties, when the Terran climate had changed. Fen thought about school and what a bore it was going to be. Fortunately, it was still some time in the future, and by then he felt sure that he would have thought of a way to avoid it.

He had questioned Penny relentlessly about his new family and discovered very little except that they were rich, a concept of which Fen had only a hazy, academic understanding, and that there were three children, one over the legal limit. This, too, was a strange idea to one who came from an underpopulated planet where large families were encouraged. He felt a brief pang of nostalgia for his twelve siblings, one of them just hatched, then fell to wondering again what it would all be like.

Human beings of every conceivable size and shape crowded the platform as the train slid to a stop. Fen was particularly enchanted by the fat ones, since neither he nor any other Chelan could manage to put on so much as an extra ounce. There was a woman in a tentlike pink tunic that failed to conceal a veritable mountain of fat. She was accompanied by an even more enormous man and two small but globular children. Fen reflected that on Chela these interesting people would have been glued permanently to the ground on which they stood because of the higher gravity there.

Fascinating people, clothing (so much of it!), houses, trees, vehicles . . . and then he saw another dog. Fen caught his breath and felt the slight but distinct rise in temperature that accompanied a change in the color of his skin. With a great effort of will, he closed his eyes and forced his body to slow down. He must not change color on the train. "Wait until you feel at home and accepted," his instructor had said. "No one expects you to stay grey forever, but try not to startle strangers, especially those in charge of moving vehicles."

After a long moment Fen opened his eyes and was pleased to see only the slightest suffusion of green, already fading from his skin. In control again, he turned his head and gazed out the window at the dog, which had come very close to the monorail car apparently to mark it with urine. It was a magnificent creature, very different from the tiny mutt in the spaceport, but Fen knew his dogs. "Labrador," he said aloud, and then sat drinking with his eyes the noble head, the silky coat, the plumed tail.

Penny, perhaps already disturbed by the stopping of the train, was jolted awake by the sound of his voice. "What? Help! Oh God, is this White Plains?"

Fen laid a hand on her arm, ignoring the slight shudder that always seemed to run through her at his touch, and pointed to the station sign. "New Canaan," he said.

Penny sank back with a sigh of relief. "Don't let me sleep more than another ten minutes," she said. "We have to get off at the next stop."

"I'm not going to let you sleep at all," Fen said indignantly. "I've thought up about a hundred questions in the last hour." Penny moaned and opened her eyes a fraction of an inch. "First and most important," he went on, "will my new family have a dog?"

"I haven't the foggiest," Penny said. "Probably. A dog or a cat or a bird. Maybe all three. Everyone has pets."

"Everyone has pets," Fen repeated stupidly. Why had no one mentioned this fascinating fact, or was it taken so for granted that it wasn't thought worth mentioning?

"Well, not everyone," Penny said. "Some people just hate animals so much they are prepared to ignore all the medical advice. Some people don't even have plants. But I doubt you would have been placed with such an abnormal family. What would be the point? I just never thought to ask about pets. The place could be a zoo for all I know."

"That," Fen said, "would surely be too much to ask."

# three

Daria was in a hurry when she got to her room with the loaded food trolley, and also in a temper, although it was pointless to be mad at Tim. Tim was sometimes helpful, but never in response to a direct plea. He was more likely to trot up beside her when she was carrying a huge tub of yams and take it out of her arms—that kind of thing—impulsive chivalry, nothing you could count on.

Even though they would not be fed until evening, she went first to the binturongs' enclosure to remove the two boxes she had given them to play with the night before. Pulling aside the flap in the plastic curtain in front of their cage released a wave of heavy musk into the room. It was not a pleasant smell, and there was a lot of it. Keeping it from escaping into the rest of the house had been an engineering challenge that Roger had met with nearly total success. Daria didn't mind the smell or even really notice it very much. It went with the binturongs, and the binturongs were the love of her life at the moment.

Some people still called them bearcats, though they were neither bears nor cats and didn't even look like cats. They were, perhaps, a little bearlike with their shaggy, dark grey coats and bright little eyes, though a bear would have wondered what to do with a tail that was almost as big as it was. The binturongs used this magnificent appendage as an extra paw while climbing, and young ones could even hang by their tails. Daria's pair were named Saskia and Igor. The Russian names had been some keeper's whim, since their lineage was strictly Bronx and Cleveland, their ancestral home the jungles of Indonesia. Saskia was bigger than her mate—a burly lady with heavy, coarse fur and a thick, bushy tail. Both of them were peering at Daria over the edge of their nest, their pointed noses twitching hopefully. "I suppose you think you can have a bedtime snack," Daria said, "just because you're expecting." She gave half a banana to Saskia and the other half to Igor, who was looking anxious about being left out, and heaved the boxes out through the flap. Left alone, the binturongs curled up inside their tails and went to sleep.

Daria gave a thawed rat to the boa, who regarded it languidly. "Live ones are supposed to be on the way," she said. "Meanwhile, eat that or go without. It's all one to me."

Pulling the food trolley close so that she could reach it from inside the monkey enclosure, Daria backed in carrying a brimming tray of chopped greens for the tamarins. She stood on a tree stump, stretching to reach the old tray and replace it with the new. Elfie, the mother of the clan, hopped on her shoulder and then into the tray. This had an unbalancing effect, but Elfie didn't weigh much, and Daria was expecting it. Clutching a leaf of kale, Elfie peered over the edge of the tray. She had a tiny black face comically adorned with a puffy white mustache and a tail that was almost four times the length of her sleek little body. Daria put a tray of crushed monkey chow on another platform and hung a bunch of overripe bananas from a branch. The used trays would go out into the hall to be collected, washed, and sterilized by Esfor.

Daria watched as the seven other members of the tamarin family, whistling excitedly, leaped from the upper branches to pounce on the food. She watched for pleasure, since there is nothing more fun than a cageful of monkeys, and she watched with what was gradually becoming a trained zookeeper's eye for any of the myriad small signs that might mean disease or injury. Mustached tamarins bred well in captivity and were no longer on the endangered list, but it would be years until their wild population even approached what it had been before the environmental crash. For now all seemed to be well with Daria's small colony, and she suspected that Elfie was pregnant.

On the floor of the aviary, the dwarf mongooses were still asleep in their simulated termite mound, and the hornbills were taking turns sliding down from the top of the mound past the holes that led to the mongoose bedchamber. As each sliding hornbill passed the mouth of a tunnel, it uttered a loud "wok." "There's nothing to hunt, you silly birds," Daria said. She slipped into the enclosure and dumped a pail of crickets into the grass. The thump of the pail finally brought the mongooses, yawning and stretching, out of their holes, though they were still in no hurry to start chasing crickets. They groomed themselves and each other, trotted off to their toilet mound, and then one by one stretched their small brown bodies up against a leaning branch to mark it with their scent. Like putting up a flag every morning, Daria thought, or a "no trespassing" sign. The hornbills had started to hunt crickets on their own, and soon the mongooses joined them, plunging into the grass, pouncing and crunching while the birds caught the ones that got away.

Daria put fresh fruit and seeds on trays in the tree for the other birds and watched for a moment as they gathered at the feast. Rare but not shy, the Bali mynas got there first. They were elegant white members of the starling family with black-tipped wings and tails. The soft crests of the males lifted and sank as they fed. And there, ridiculous and utterly appealing, came the tiny, blue-crowned hanging parrots, striding up the tree trunk with steps that would have been long for a bird three times their size. The hardworking golden weavers left the building of their intricate nests, and the beautiful violet touraco, the largest of Daria's birds but by far the most timid, peered from a thick mat of foliage to see if it was safe to come out and eat.

Squeezing out of the aviary, Daria paused to look at her

watch. Foxes, turtles, and then outdoors for the llamas and the water birds. She saw that she still had half an hour—enough for these chores, if not for a change of clothes and breakfast.

The foxes were seminocturnal, but she still liked to feed them in the morning and keep them up a while so she could enjoy them. They were fennecs, a tiny breed of desert fox with thick cream-colored fur and truly enormous ears flaring above their little pointed faces. Lured by the scent of food, the dog fox emerged from the thorn brake in front of their cave, but there was no sign of the vixen. That was the first odd thing Daria noticed. The second was the faint mewing sound that came from behind the thorns. She almost dropped the tray of chopped meat, grubs, and fruit. Not the binturong but the fennec fox had given birth this morning. Obviously she had miscalculated.

Forgetting everything—the other animals and even the arriving alien—Daria ran for a flashlight. Then she shoved the food tray into the corner of the cage as far as possible from the cave and crawled in after it. Eyeing her warily, the dog fox selected a fat grub, which he threw up in the air, caught, chewed, and swallowed. The second one he took behind the pile of rocks that formed the cave. Daria dropped to her stomach and began to wriggle under the thorns, adding several more tears to her already ragged tunic and a few to her skin. The mewing was now quite loud, as was the thumping of Daria's heart. She saw the mouth of the cave through the tangled branches and slowed her progress to about a quarter of an inch per wiggle. Finally she was able to peer into the dark cavity beneath the rocks. There was a glint of watchful eyes, the shadowy outline of pointed ears, but that was all.

Having brought the flashlight, Daria was now afraid to use it, but she knew she must check the condition of mother and babies. Besides, she was dying to see them. "Snippet," she whispered. "Snippet, my love. Did you have some beautiful kits? Aren't you the clever girl?" The vixen was tame, or had been until now. Slowly, as if caution could reduce the impact of the light, Daria pushed the button on the flash. It was a dim bulb, designed for just such occasions. Even so, the small cavity seemed to explode with light. A brief tremor ran over the little vixen's body, but that was all. She lay still, head up, ears forward, staring at her human friend while at her teats four tiny, blind kits mewed and sucked.

Daria gave a sigh of relief and happiness. This was one of those times that made it all not only worthwhile but transcendent. At that moment she knew that there was no place she would rather be than here, flat on her stomach under a thorn bush, no company she would rather keep than that of this shy mother and her newborn young. Slowly she stretched out her hand until she could stroke that special place behind the vixen's ears. Snippet whined softly and licked the caressing hand.

It was some time before Daria became aware that she had an agonizing crick in her neck and that a certain amount of blood was drying on her arms and back. She also realized that someone was knocking on her door. From the sound of it, whoever was knocking had been at it for some time. The family was well trained to knock and wait for Daria to open the door. In case they forgot, there was a large sign that read, "Never open this door! Dangerous animals may be loose inside." The problem now was to get to the door before it caved in. She was damn well not going to shout with her head in a cave full of newborn fox kits. Daria began a slow and painful exit from the thorn bush and finally out the front flap of the cage. She jerked the door open, and her mother nearly fell into the room.

Mother and daughter stood looking at each other with equal disapproval. Gloria Wells was dressed as if for some major media event—perhaps the preview of one of her hypertext romances—in a shimmering sleeveless tunic of pale green silk and high-heeled sandals. Her dark gold hair was wound in an intricate knot on top of her head. "Do you have to make such a racket?" Daria began.

"Look at you!" her mother cried. "Our guest is due in less than five minutes, and you look as if you've been dismembered by a grizzly bear."

"Holy herrings," Daria said. "Would you believe I forgot?"

"No," said her mother. "I wouldn't believe it. Not even knowing you as well as I do. How often do we have a visitor from another planet? Throw something big on over all that blood and brush your hair. I'll pretend I don't know you."

Daria, rummaging dutifully in her closet for some roomy and not too unbecoming garment, still had time to feel exasperated with her mother. "I don't see why we have to make such an impression," she grumbled. "It's not like he's really a visitor, Mom. He's coming to live with us, as I understand it, so he might as well see us as we are. I don't suppose he has the option of taking one look at me and going instantly back to Chela."

"Well do something to lessen the shock," Gloria said. "I'll leave you to it, since I can't bear to watch."

Daria yanked a long-sleeved tunic out of the closet, stripped off her gory rags, and pulled it over her head. "Mirror, please," she said to the computer, which obligingly silvered its monitor screen so she could brush her thick tangle of dark curls. The computer had been programmed not to comment, and this was just as well, Daria thought. There was a scratch on the bridge of her nose and a scrape on one cheek. Dark eyes stared out of a thin brown face that was a shade too intense and already, perhaps, beginning to develop frown lines. "I'll have to do," Daria said. She pulled a pair of thong sandals from the chaos of nets, leashes, and feed pails under the table and put them on. Then, instead of following her mother down the hall to the living room, she turned and went out the door that led from her room into the garden.

# four

Daria glanced guiltily at the crowd of geese, cranes, and ducks clamoring for breakfast at the kitchen door and slipped around the corner of the house to the front garden. Without really knowing why, she wanted to be the first to see the alien visitor. I'll just take a peek when he starts up the path, she thought. Then I can dash inside and join the others. A long path wound through flowering hedges to the road, and she walked slowly along it until she was out of sight of the front window, where the rest of her family waited. The garden was very still, and even the hungry water birds seemed for the moment to have fallen silent. Daria stopped halfway to the road, listening for a footstep or the slam of a scooter door, feeling the sudden acceleration of her heart as she strained to see in the patterned light and shade the arrival of the stranger.

Fen's head and shoulders appeared before the rest of him and seemed to glide ghostlike along the top of the hedgerow. Even prepared as she was for something very tall, Daria was startled by his height, which was slightly more than seven feet—not unheard-of for a human being, but still remarkable and made more so by the seeming fragility of his arms and upper body. He was an agreeable shade of medium grey and appeared to be entirely unclothed. All this was the impression of a moment, for Fen was moving fast and now came around the last bend of the path and into plain view. Daria could see that he was not totally naked but wore a sort of bath sarong from waist to mid-thigh. A young woman who seemed to be in the last stages of exhaustion trudged in his wake, carrying a large suitcase.

At the sight of Daria, Fen came to an abrupt halt, and Penny nearly ran into him. He adopted the formal greeting posture of his people: ramrod straight, head thrown back, arms halfway extended at his sides with the hands turned out, palms down. Elegant and formidable, Daria thought. Clothes would be redundant on this young prince from outer space. "Greetings from the Republic of Chela," Fen said. "Are you one of my new siblings?"

"I may be," Daria said. "Hi. Welcome. I'm Daria Wells."

"Fen, at your service. And this is Penny, who has brought me here from the spaceport."

"Hi, Penny. Come on inside. You look bushed. I hope you didn't walk from the station. It's doable, but only just."

"I fear I became overexcited and told the driver to let us

off too soon," Fen said. "In front of a house called Callahan, in fact."

"That's about a quarter of a mile," Daria said. "Poor you, and with a suitcase, too."

"We will soon revive, especially if fed fairly quickly," Fen said.

Daria laughed. "That should be no problem. I'm sure we have something you can eat, although nobody told us what."

"Feeding him will be the least of your problems, believe me," said Fen's escort. "Don't let him keep you up all night. He has curiosity like a disease." She was backing slowly toward the road as she spoke, leaving the suitcase stranded in the path.

"But that's good," Daria protested. "Of course he's curious. Wouldn't you be? You're not leaving, I hope. There's no way you can pick up a scooter on the road, and besides we're going to have tons of stuff to ask you."

Penny stopped. "You can ask him anything you want. He's not shy, and I really do have to go somewhere and get some sleep."

"Please stay a little, Penny," Fen said. "I have not had time to thank you or to say a proper farewell. Come inside with us. Nice Daria will give us food, and you will feel much livelier."

"That's what you've been telling me ever since we met," Penny said, beginning to drag herself back up the path, "and for me it stopped working along about midnight last night. He eats to stay awake," she said to Daria. "I mean, we do that, too, but there are limits, right? After a while food just makes you want to lie down and digest and never get up again."

"Well, come along," Daria said. "I'll get the suitcase, or Fen will." She looked up at the tall alien, and he smiled a rather overwhelming smile, disclosing double rows of small but pointed teeth. He made no move to pick up his luggage. Daria shrugged. If women were the beasts of burden on Chela, this was an issue that could wait. She picked up the suitcase, which seemed to be empty, and started toward the house, Fen by her side, Penny straggling behind.

"You don't seem to have brought much," Daria said, "unless your clothes are awfully light."

"I brought nothing. The suitcase is for souvenirs."

Daria stopped and stared at him again—his great expanse of silvery grey skin, the minimal wrap around his loins, and, now she saw it for the first time, the curious amulet shaped like an animal tooth that hung on a gold chain around his neck. "You didn't bring anything? Not a stitch besides what you stand up in?"

"We have a very warm climate," Fen explained, "and we understood that you do also, at least in the season that has now begun. Except for a few cumbersome and tedious ceremonial robes, we do not concern ourselves with clothing."

Daria grinned. Lily was going to love this. "Only problem is," she said, "there are going to be places you'll want to go where clothes are a must."

"I told him that," Penny said. "He thinks just because he's an alien, he can wear what he pleases."

"I count upon the well-known courtesy of your race," said Fen, and Daria laughed.

"Somebody gave us some good publicity," she said. "Never mind. The next thing is to meet the family, get some food into you, and plop Penny into a deep armchair, so let's go."

By this time their little group was within sight of the house, and Gloria was at the door to meet them. "You must be our exchange student," she cried. "Welcome to our humble home, and come meet the rest of the family. Daria, I see, has already introduced herself."

Daria could tell that her mother was far from pleased to be a mere second in the greeting department, but she was making up for it in cordiality as she led the way into the living room. Tim wore a pair of dark glasses and the air of the man who has seen everything. Lily had assumed a statuesque pose against a potted palm near the hall door.

"Greetings, Earthy family," said Fen. "I am Fen. In the name of the Republic of Chela, I thank you for your prospective hospitality."

Daria thought this a hard line to follow, but her mother was at home in social situations. "We are so happy to have you," she said. "Please sit down. You must be tired after your long journey. And are you Miss Mackleby?"

"I am," said Penny, "and I really must be on my way."

"Don't even think of it. We have so much to ask you. Have the big chair. You look exhausted."

Penny sank into the chair with a small whimper, and Tim strolled over to Fen.

"Fen, meet Tim," Daria said.

"I am most pleased," said Fen. "Why do you cover your eyes in this agreeably dim place?"

Tim grinned. "Because it's cool, man."

"Cool?" Fen said, and looked around for help.

"Tim, please try to talk like a normal human being," Gloria said. "You know you can, and it would be a help. Poor Fen will have trouble enough living his life in a second language without you to muddle him. Your English is wonderful, by the way, Fen."

"Thank you," said Fen. "It is supposed to be adequate, but I am most anxious to learn the current colloquialisms."

"Then don't listen to Tim," said Lily. "He lives half the time in the last century and has a really bizarre vocabulary."

Fen turned his amber gaze upon Lily and treated her to the full splendor of his smile. Lily shrank and edged toward the entrance to the hall. "Are you my other sister?" he asked.

"If that's the way you want to put it," Lily muttered. Fen was advancing upon her now, and Daria wondered if she would stand her ground or disgrace them all by fleeing down the hall.

"You are very beautiful," he said. "May I touch your hair?"

"Not just now," Lily said. "I just washed it. It's full of electricity."

"Later then, when the danger has decreased?"

"We'll see about that," said Lily. "Why don't you just go

and sit down for now? Take the weight off your feet."

"As it happens, there isn't much weight on my feet," Fen said. "Far too little at times. As for sitting down, I am much too interested in your wonderful house. Please let me examine its artifacts, and please get me something to *eat.*"

"Mom," Daria said, "you're failing as a hostess."

"Would you like a sandwich, Fen?" Gloria asked. "We don't know what you eat. Ham and cheese?"

"Perhaps he's a vegetarian," said Daria, who had, several years ago, become unwilling to consume anything too obviously animal in origin.

"We are omnivores," Fen said grandly. "Bring what you like, nice Mom, and, if possible, some mildly intoxicating beverage to go with it."

Tim laughed. "A man after my own heart. Bring him a beer, Mom, and one for me while you're at it."

"Tim, I really don't think... It's too early in the day for you, and how do I know what beer would do to a Chelan? I am, after all, in loco parentis, so to speak."

"I have heard excellent reports of beer," said Fen. "Please bring me some, and several sandwiches of whatever sort you think best." His voice, which was agreeably low-pitched, was as polite as ever, but there was something about it and about the imperious gaze of his yellow eyes that gave one pause. Daria thought the color of his skin had darkened slightly.

"Well, maybe just a small glass. Penny, what do you think? That's a big help. She's out like a light."

"Perhaps I can assist with the food," Fen said. There was

now no mistaking the slight edge of menace in his voice.

"Nonsense," Gloria cried. "We just push a few buttons, you know."

"Excellent," Fen said, and began to prowl around the living room while she went to get the food. He examined every object in the most minute detail, and it occurred to Daria, who had never thought the contents of the living room very interesting, that even the most mundane object, if seen for the first time, could be quite fascinating. There was a ciggo box, for example, carved from the bole of a redwood tree, and a crystal ashtray on the coffee table. Fen seemed less interested in technology than in common household things and gave the media center only a glance, passing on to a pair of rather scruffy shoes that had escaped the attentions of Gloria and Esfor. These he picked up and studied with a condescending smile. "Shoes are one thing you'll never get me into," said Fen, as he put them back under the couch.

The next thing that caught his attention was a set of keys on the table by the front door, and now he seemed really baffled. He held them up, letting the thin slivers of coded plastic slide through his fingers.

"Keys," Tim said. "Are yours so very different?"

"Keys," said Fen. "Keys. I know the word, but the concept eludes me."

"The concept of keys eludes you?"

"I understand that they are used to make doors difficult, if not impossible, to open. You lock a door so that another person may not enter. Then, with the same key, you open it again."

"Right on the button," Tim said.

"Why?"

The question hung on the air for a moment as if the answer was so obvious that no one could think of words to express it. Finally Tim said, "Well, look, old man. We lock doors so other people don't come in and take things that belong to us."

The Chelan still frowned. Daria found it difficult to see what his problem was. "Think of it this way," she said. "Suppose we left the door open, and we all went out..." Fen nodded encouragingly. "Well, someone could just walk in and take—oh, I don't know—that box maybe or some of Lily's jewelry or my microscope or Tim's percussion instruments or, you know, whatever that person fancied or thought was valuable."

"And so?" Fen said.

"And so that would be bad, and so we lock our doors," Daria finished rather crossly.

"But if no one locked doors, you could go and get even more interesting things from other houses."

"But we like our own things," Lily cried. She had edged back into the family circle while still keeping an escape route open to the hall. The reference to her jewelry, some of which she had designed herself, must have prompted this outburst.

"This is a society in need of reform," Fen said, and

again there was something implacable in his manner, as if he might have been about to add, "starting with you," or some such disagreeable sentiment.

Happily, at this point Gloria returned with a tray on which a glass of beer and a large ham sandwich were prettily displayed on a fringed napkin. Fen leaped for the food with such enthusiasm that for a moment he left the ground entirely and tapped his head on the ceiling.

"Do you have much stronger gravity on Chela?" Tim asked.

"Mush," Fen said. His mouth was already full of ham sandwich, and Daria shuddered at the thought of all those pointed teeth rending the flesh of some hapless pig.

Both the sandwich and the beer disappeared in something under a minute. "Delicious," the Chelan said, and looked hopefully at Gloria.

"We will all have lunch together quite soon," she said, "and tonight perhaps my husband will make a real dinner. Unlike most of us modern folk, he is quite a marvelous cook."

"Can he make cakes and pies?" Fen wanted to know.

"You name it, Dad can cook it," Tim said. "So have no fear of starvation, my friend. You've landed in pig heaven." Fen gave a happy sigh.

Daria had been looking hard at their visitor during this exchange—looking with the eyes of a zoologist. But you didn't have to be a zoologist to see that something very strange was taking place. She caught her breath, and her eyes bulged. There was no mistaking it now. The Chelan was changing color. All over, from head to foot, his medium grey skin was becoming suffused with pink, like the coming of dawn on a foggy morning. She glanced at the rest of the family and saw that they, too, were staring at this curious phenomenon.

For Lily it must have been the last straw. "I'm getting out of here. It's too weird," she muttered, and fled down the hall.

Fen watched her departure with regret. "Tell me what I have done to offend beautiful Lily," he said, "and I will promise never to do it again."

"You haven't exactly done anything," Daria said, "but, Fen, look at yourself. You've gone all pink. We don't do that, and Lily is very conventional."

Fen looked down at his rosy limbs and frowned. Daria thought that at that moment the whole effect faded a little. "I am sorry," he said. "At the thought of all that good food, I lost control. We were warned that you might find such transformations threatening."

"I think it's a very becoming shade," Gloria said. "Please don't give it another thought."

"But how do you do it?" Daria cried. "It's the most fascinating thing I've ever seen. I mean, some of our lizards change color, but you're nothing like a lizard, are you?"

"Not so far as I know," Fen said rather stiffly. His pink color was definitely fading now, but not back to grey. He was becoming instead a sickly shade of ocher, and Daria was alarmed.

"I'm sorry," she said. "My beastly curiosity. That was really pretty rude."

Fen drew a long-fingered hand across his forehead. "Your curiosity is natural," he said. "It is only that I am suddenly very tired." He swayed slightly and caught himself by putting his hand on the ceiling.

"Let me show you to your room," Gloria said hastily.

"Please," Fen said, and smiling a groggy smile, he followed her down the hall.

"So much for a formal thank-you and farewell," came Penny's voice from the depths of the chair.

"He got very tired very suddenly, like a small child," Daria said. "Maybe Mom was right and the beer wasn't a good idea."

"Don't be dense," Tim said. "If you had zapped through space and landed on a new planet and ridden on a train all night and met a pack of new people, a beer and a sandwich would put you out, too."

"I suppose so. God, I wish I knew what makes him change color like that."

"Change color?" Penny said. "What on earth are you talking about?"

"He didn't do it on the train?"

"Didn't do what on the train?"

"Change from grey to almost shocking pink for starters, and I suspect he has a whole rainbow in his repertory. You couldn't have missed it with all that bare skin, unless you were asleep the whole time."

"I was certainly not asleep the whole time," Penny said. "Why do you think I'm such a wreck? He only let me sleep for about an hour at a time, and when I wasn't asleep, I was answering questions. It's my fault, of course. We should have popped onto a plane or a rocket like all the rest of the exchange students and their escorts. But no. I had to be creative. I thought it would be educational for him to come on the train and see a few things."

"And obviously it was," Daria said. "I think you did an excellent thing and should have a medal for it."

"Never mind the medal," Penny said. "Just let me get home to my own bed. Can you call a scooter to take me to the station?"

"One of us will drive you," Daria said. "Won't we, Tim?"

"You go," Tim said. "You need the practice."

"I've still got animals to feed. I wonder if Fen likes animals. What a bummer if he doesn't."

"Animals!" Penny cried. "He's obsessed with animals. What he wanted to know most about you was whether you had any pets. I hope you do, because if you don't, he'll be dragging some mangy cur home on a rope before he's been here a day."

Daria laughed. "He won't have to do that. We don't exactly have pets, but at last count there were forty-five—wait, make that forty-nine—animals on the premises. That's not counting the migrant birds and the bats."

Penny's eyes bulged. "You're kidding me." Daria shook her head. "He'll go bananas," Penny said. "He'll think he's died and gone to heaven. Wow."

"At last a kindred spirit for my poor sister," Tim said. "The rest of us aren't really into the menagerie thing."

"Did he talk about the animals on Chela?" Daria asked.

"Nobody knows what they're like. Except for a lot of insects and some ratlike things, nobody has ever seen a Chelan animal."

Penny yawned. "I'm sure all you have to do is ask," she said, but not while I'm around, thank you very much. We all have our obsessions, and mine happens to be with sleep. Never mind driving me if it's a problem. I can hitch."

"Oh, come on," Tim said. "I was only teasing Daria. A trip to the station with her is the last thing you need in your dilapidated state. Let's go."

"That's a vile slander," Daria said. "But thanks. Bye, Penny. Sorry we didn't get a chance to talk some more. Thanks for bringing us our very own alien."

"Enjoy," said Penny, and followed Tim out the door.

Daria watched them go around the corner of the house to the carport. She could hear the birds still yelling for their breakfasts, but she sat staring into space and thinking about the strange being who had entered their lives so suddenly and found them so unprepared.

"This is stupid," Daria said to the empty room. She went over to the computer console and punched into the Net. In a matter of seconds she had all the files on Chela at her fingertips. She glanced rapidly through the basic information about the planet: larger than Earth, higher gravity, three moons, four small continents in a lot of ocean, no polar caps, climate hot but livable in the temperate zones. It was a beautiful place, too, and Daria lingered over the pictures of mountains, forests, and seacoasts. The forests particularly arrested her eye. They looked dense and primeval, extravagantly lush but also forbidding, like the jungles of Amazonia a hundred years ago. "Well, that's one place the animals are," Daria said. "We just can't see them."

# five

Fen was relieved when, after a certain amount of fussing, Gloria left him alone in his room. Too tired to explore it in detail, he did observe that the bed, though much too short, was wide and inviting. He could sleep diagonally and longed to do just that, but there was something even more important that he must do first. Filya would be wondering what had become of him.

He put his suitcase on a chair and rummaged through its sparse collection of monorail souvenirs (napkins, a small towel, a ciggotray, and a handful of postcards Penny had bought him at one of their stops) until he found the only thing he had brought from Chela. It had been decided, pretty much at the last minute, that it would be essential for the nine young visitors to be able to communicate with one another from their widely separated temporary homes on Earth. The fact that this had not been part of the original plan just showed, some said, how harebrained a plan it was. More probably the truly staggering cost of the communicators, which were a recent marvel of Chelan technology, had given the sponsors pause.

With a sigh, Fen let the annoying bath sarong fall to the floor and sank onto the bed. The device had only two visible components. One, which resembled a trumpet bell the size of a pea, took care of sending and receiving sound. The visual element was more remarkable, consisting as it did of an elastic monitor screen. The size of a large postage stamp at its smallest, it could be kneaded and stretched to a square of more than two feet.

Fen settled for a six-inch screen, propped it on his chest, and flipped it on. Since it was already set for Filya's wavelength, it didn't matter whether she was in Rome (which she was) or Siberia. In a blink the delicate silvery form of his friend, and perhaps someday his mate, filled the little screen. As yet unaware that she was being called, Filya gazed pensively through a long window. There was a balcony outside crowded with flowering plants, a red-tiled roof across from it, and beyond that what Fen guessed was the tower of a religious institution. Both the roof and the tower were clearly very old, unlike anything he had seen so far in America.

"Filya," Fen whispered, "Filya, you ice maiden, you. How can you be so grey when Fen is calling you?"

She started, then reached into a small bag that hung from her wrist and produced another communicator. Fen was gratified to see a wonderful flush of lavender tinged with rose spread from the peak of her high forehead to the tips of her slender, slightly prehensile toes. This color almost immediately darkened to a rather threatening deep purple as she remembered how angry she was. "Fen!" she cried, tugging wrathfully at the edges of her monitor, "how could you leave me so long in suspense? Where have you been? I have called everyone for news of you, which has been very inconvenient and embarrassing. My new family thinks I am going to spend all my time locked in my room, and our friends think I am being silly, although they, too, are beginning to worry. You are an awful color, by the way. Is anything wrong?"

"I'm tired," Fen said defensively. "You would be, too. I came here by train, which took a whole day and night, and I managed to stay awake the whole time."

"By train?" Filya said. "How quaint."

"It was incredibly interesting and worth any amount of physical depletion."

"Lucky you. All I saw, besides this very small, very old city where I will live, were clumps of boring little buildings on the road from the airport. This is where, if you can believe it, the people who aren't good at doing anything are made to live."

"I saw those, too," Fen said, "but also big white houses with windmills and beautiful trees, cows and horses, and a marsh full of wading birds."

"Oh, Fen. I could die for such a trip. My family hardly ever leaves the city. They say they have everything here, so why should they travel to other places? I will try to persuade them after we know each other better. And, of course, I can look at things on the Net. They say I can see anything I want to see just sitting in a chair."

"Are they fat?"

"No, but they only eat three times a day."

Fen was genuinely concerned. "I hope they have food slots," he said. "I have been told that I can eat whenever I want to."

"Yes, thank the Powers, they do. Mostly one can get a thing called pizza, which is fabulously delicious. Possibly I will even put on some weight."

"And I will become the only male on Chela to have a fat bride."

"You hope," Filya said.

"Don't be contrary," Fen said. "We've been over this a thousand times."

"On Chela."

"On Chela, of course, where else?"

"Don't you feel we might be different when we get back, Fen? Don't you think we might be changed somehow?"

"I don't see why," he said. "And besides, you promised me on the night of the three moons. Filya, are you listening to me?"

She was leaning forward and gazing with a tender smile not at the monitor, but at something near the window of her room. "Are you ready to turn yellow with envy?" Filya asked. "Unless, of course, you have one, too. Wait a second. Don't say a word." She bent down and made a ridiculous kissing sound. Then, switching from Chelan to Italian, she called, *"Micetta, micetta,"* and a lithe ginger cat jumped into her lap. It stretched a curious paw toward her monitor, so for a moment all Fen could see was a blur. Then it sat back and gazed at him. It had large amber eyes, almost Chelan eyes, set in a tiny triangular face. Filya's long fingers stroked its striped head and rubbed behind its ears.

Fen was speechless with envy and desire. His friend had what he wanted more than anything else—a household animal, a pet—and in his new home he had seen not a sign of animal life. It wasn't fair, but it would be impossible to feign indifference. No Chelan would credit such a posture for an instant. "A cat," he said. "You have a cat. Girl, you were born lucky."

"But Fen, pets are common," Filya said. "Doesn't your family have a pet? If they don't, you should ask for one."

"I will. Believe me. But what if they don't like animals?" Both Chelans were silent for a moment contemplating the enormity of such an attitude.

"I wouldn't worry," Filya said finally. "That's hardly likely, is it? And besides, if you are in the country, as you seem to be from what I can see out your window, there will be wild animals you can tame. Probably you are better off than I am. You just don't see it yet. Fen, I think you should get some sleep. Even talking to me has not improved your color, and it's making me rather ill to look at you."

"Thanks," Fen said. "Just what I need to hear."

"Don't be ridiculous," said his (perhaps) future mate.

"Get some sleep. Probably when you wake up, there will be animals looking in your window."

There was a click, and Fen's monitor went dark. He stared at it numbly for a moment, then shoved the whole thing under his pillow, turned his face to the wall, and immediately lost consciousness.

# six

Daria, too, having given the outdoor birds a rather hasty meal, was engaged in communication with a distant friend, although in her case the distance was a mere twenty miles. She was talking to Giovanna Ferrante, the director of the Hudson Valley Ark, an enormous facility for the breeding of endangered species located just north of Peekskill on the Hudson River. On the big screen in Daria's room, the tall, energetic figure of her mentor could be seen prowling through the confusion of nets, cages, gloves, poles, hip boots, food supplements, and computer printouts that her office comprised. A handsome cockatoo rode on Giovanna's shoulder and busied itself with pulling the pins out of her massive grey bun. There were rumors at the Ark that Giovanna's hair was in itself a special habitat; opinions varied as to its inhabitants.

"So your little fennec has four beautiful babies," Giovanna said. "Congratulations. She's been getting her supplements, I hope. Calcium, extra vitamins, iron, all that good stuff?"

Daria sighed. "What do you think, Giovanna?"

"I think she has."

"And you're right."

"Of course I am. Still, I think I would like to see this little family for myself—just because I would like to see it, you understand. Who can grow tired of baby foxes?"

The thought of crawling under the thorn bush and into the fennecs' cave with a video camera was more than Daria could contemplate at the moment. "Could it wait until tomorrow, Giovanna?" she said. "We're having a particularly hairy day."

"All days are hairy, as you put it, in the life of a keeper."

"Yes, but some are hairier than others. We're running a special event at the moment known as the exchange student from outer space comes to Westchester and invades the house of Wells."

"Knowing that English is only my second language, Daria, perhaps you could express yourself more simply," said Giovanna in her near-perfect English.

"English hasn't been your second language for fifty years," Daria said. "It's the idea that eludes you."

"So elucidate."

"I plan to." It was Daria's turn to prowl. She got up from the big chair where she usually sat curled up for her chats with Giovanna and started to roam restlessly around the room while Giovanna perched on a stool and fixed her protégée with bright black eyes.

"Our remarkable mom," Daria began, "without asking the rest of us, decided it would be a feather in her cap to have one of the exchange students from Chela, and somehow she managed to bring it off. He arrived this morning."

"*Per bacco!*" Giovanna leaped from her stool, and the cockatoo fled with an indignant squawk to the top of a pile of crates. "You have a Chelan in your house? Daria, this is electrifying news!"

"Isn't it?" Daria said. "It also explains why I am a little off my usual routine and even a nest of tiny fennecs fails to completely rivet my attention. Giovanna, he is strange."

"What would you expect?"

"I expected him to be strange, and, of course, I've seen lots of pictures. Everybody has. But I didn't expect him to change color. All the pictures have shown a fairly even grey complexion. I just wasn't prepared for shocking pink, which is what he turned when we gave him a ham sandwich and a beer."

"Before or after ingesting this dubious meal?" Giovanna wanted to know.

"After, I think, but it was when we were talking about food, about what a super cook Dad is and how he would never have to go hungry in our house."

"So it could be emotional or alimentary or both."

"If you want to put it like that."

"I must see him immediately."

"You can't," Daria said. "He's dead to the world, poor

thing, and please don't peek into the guest room. I suspect you could without much difficulty."

Giovanna laughed. "*Cara,* yours is the only door on which I have to knock."

"Sorry about that," Daria said, "but you know how I feel." In the early days of her association with the Ark, she had, with the help of Tim, who was a wizard at this sort of thing, installed several quite impenetrable passwords in her system that prevented not only Giovanna but everyone else from viewing her room without her consent. Giovanna had argued that this was not safe. Daria might be bitten by a poisonous snake or mauled by a binturong, and no one would be the wiser. Daria had countered that she had no poisonous snakes and was capable of escaping from a thirty-pound binturong before being rendered unconscious from loss of blood or whatever. It was a teenage thing, she had explained, this matter of privacy, and she didn't expect it to change in the near future.

"But you will arrange a meeting when he wakes up," Giovanna persisted.

"I'll try," Daria said. "It depends, I think, on Fen. That's his name, by the way. He's very—I don't know if this is right—very willful, Giovanna. You have the feeling that if you plan something, and he plans something else, it will be what he plans that happens."

"Be that as it may," the zoologist said, "you have a matchless opportunity here to do a field study on a unique species. Observe, observe, observe, *cara mia.* Take reams of notes. I will be watching for them day and night."

"Don't I know it," Daria said. Her zoology note pad was directly on-line to Giovanna, so anything she jotted down—the mating of a mongoose, the fact that the binturongs were unaccountably tired of raisins, and now, it would seem, the behavior of her house guest—would immediately be known to Giovanna, and, potentially, to the entire zoological establishment. It was unnerving at best. Daria, like most other teenagers and many adults, had a second diary that took the form of a small book of lined paper and a pencil stub.

"This color change is fascinating," Giovanna went on. "What possible evolutionary purpose could be served for a humanoid species? Camouflage? Not likely for so advanced an animal. Communication of emotion, like your chameleons? Redundant in a creature that possesses the power of speech. And why have all the Chelans observed by scientists been the same boring color?"

"I haven't a clue," Daria said, "except he said something about forgetting to control himself. He scared Lily out of her single wit by turning that lurid shade of pink and then wanted to know what he had done to turn her off. When I explained that drastic, all-over color change was not something we did, he sort of looked down at himself in a startled way and apologized for losing control. It was like... well, like he got to feeling comfortable and happy and forgot to be grey."

"Excellent observation," Giovanna said. "I trust you recorded it."

"I didn't," Daria said mulishly. "It was a social occasion,

Giovanna. It was meeting somebody who is going to live in our house. It wasn't a field expedition to study the rare mountain wing wang." She became aware that her mentor's attention was wandering—something that often happened when she strayed from the zoological path. Giovanna was staring into the upper left window of her monitor—the one that showed the fennecs' enclosure.

"The dog fox looks anxious," Giovanna said. "He's nosing around the mouth of the cave. Why would he be worried?"

"He wouldn't, normally," Daria said. "Even if something was wrong, I don't think he would, but the beasties are full of surprises. I suppose I'd better have a look."

"Don't forget the camera," Giovanna said.

There was nothing wrong with the fox family, as Daria discovered after another agonizing wriggle under the thorns, this time with a miniature video camera slung around her neck. If she could have thought of any way Giovanna might influence the behavior of the dog fox over a distance of twenty miles, she wouldn't have put it past her. Still, grumbling and scratches aside, she was glad to see the mother and kits again. Giovanna's face, when her protégée finally emerged from the cage, was an extra reward. It had the wide-eyed look of a four-year-old gazing into a nest of baby rabbits. Not only did the great zoologist never tire of infant foxes, Daria thought, she never tired of anything in the world of animals. It was one of her great charms and made up for a lot of harassment.

"Neat, aren't they?" Daria said, unslinging the camera and combing the twigs out of her hair with her fingers.

"Neat and healthy as little horses as far as I can see. Your female binturong seems to be stirring up her nest box. What do you think?"

"I think soon," Daria said.

"Let's have a look, then."

"Let's not just now please. You know you can't tell anything by looking, and I've got a ton of outdoor chores still to do."

"Let it not be said that Giovanna Ferrante doesn't know when to sign off."

"Let it not," Daria said. "Bye, Giovanna. I'll try to give you a look at the resident alien later today."

The big screen went dark, and so, Daria knew, did all the tiny video cameras that peered into cages and tanks around her room. It was pleasant to be alone, and she allowed herself the luxury of lying back in the big chair for a few minutes and watching the weaverbirds work on their amazing nests. They were like golden arrows, darting through shafts of sunlight as they collected the long reeds and wove them into intricate hanging pouches. One little male was starting from scratch, and Daria felt the same tug at her heart she had experienced the first time she had seen one of these lovely birds select a strand and tie the first knot around a branch. She also saw that they were running out of reeds and soon would be frustrated if she didn't fetch some from the pond, so with a sigh she heaved herself out of the chair and went into the garden.

# seven

A loud tapping sound penetrated the profound sleep in which Fen had lain for more than an hour, tangled in dreams of strange dwellings and fantastic animals. He opened his eyes slowly, decided that what he saw at the window was only a continuation of his dream, and closed them again. Then Filya's teasing voice echoed in his returning consciousness: "When you wake up, there will be animals looking in your window." In an instant he was bolt upright in bed. A llama and a crane were gazing in at him; the crane was tapping on the glass with its long, sharp bill.

Still almost convinced that he was dreaming, Fen lowered his legs to the floor and slid to the edge of the bed. "A bird and a mammal," he whispered. Two of the great classes of animals on Earth stood at his window and seemed to beg for his attention.

The llama was golden brown with a white chest and belly. Dark eyes behind absurdly long lashes seemed to regard Fen with amusement. He suspected that the bird was young. It was smaller than those cranes whose pictures he had studied in the long memory sessions the exchange students had attended on Chela, and it had the ungainly quality of an adolescent, as well as an adolescent's lack of patience. As it drew back its head to strike the glass again, the llama bent its long neck and gave the bird a gentle shove as if to say, "Enough. You've got your victim's attention; now let him get his eyes open."

As Fen stared at his two visitors, he saw the girl, Daria, cross the lawn and walk away toward the trees at the end of the garden. He scrambled to his feet and snatched the bath sarong from the floor. Trembling, he opened the door that led outdoors from his room. He was a deep forest green from head to foot.

This sudden emergence of a large alien from the house was too much for the young crane. She gave an earsplitting squawk and retreated behind the broad back of the llama. Fen jumped several feet off the ground. "Don't be afraid," he mumbled, as much to himself as to the bird, which continued to make a horrendous noise. The llama, perhaps feeling that Fen was the more easily comforted of the two, nudged him gently in the chest with its velvet nose, and Fen felt his breathing slow and his trembling subside. "Llama," he said softly, "could we just possibly become friends?" The llama lifted its head and bumped him under the chin. Taking this for a good sign, Fen buried his fingers in the wool at the top of its head. He felt the dense, silky fibers of the animal's coat and the warmth of the blood that coursed beneath its skin. He felt in himself a rapture such as he had never imagined.

Daria, emerging from the woods with a handful of reeds, was arrested at the sight of the strange trio. The crane had ceased its squalling and was peering anxiously around the rump of its protector. The alien petted the llama, his amber eyes burning in his green face with the passion of a fanatic. "I guess he does like animals," Daria said, "or something. How weird!" She put the reeds down on the grass and cautiously approached the little group.

Fen was startled out of his trance and immediately on his guard. He had been taught that to show interest in animals was natural but that worship would be regarded as bizarre. "If you find yourself close to an animal and a Terran person is near, adopt a posture of casual bemusement," his instructor had said. Fen wasn't entirely clear about bemusement and suspected his instructor wasn't either, but casual was no problem. He was naturally suave. "Daria," he said, "what splendid animals you have. The llama I recognize, but what is the species of the crane?"

"It's a sandhill," Daria said. "They're rather rare, though not so much as they used to be. I'm trying to start a flock, and little Suzy here is one of my mistakes."

"How can such a beautiful creature be a mistake?" Fen asked.

"Oh, I didn't mean she wasn't a lovely crane," Daria said, "but I put her egg under a broody hen to hatch and didn't screen it off well enough, so the first thing she saw that was tall enough to make an acceptable mother was the llama. Now poor Peru has a constant avian shadow. It interferes with his work, but he's a patient old darling and puts up with it most of the time."

"Had something happened to her real mother? Why was her egg being hatched by a hen?"

"Her mother was busy sitting on another pair of eggs," Daria explained. "I always take the first-laid eggs and give them to a hen because the crane will be pretty sure to lay another pair. Sometimes I do it several times. I can get four to six chicks a year that way instead of only one or two, so it's worth doing."

"Poor mother crane," said Fen, thinking of how frantic his own mother would have been if someone had played such tricks on her—not that such a thing was even remotely likely.

"I wouldn't worry," Daria said. "She usually ends up with a baby to raise. Do you like birds? If you take that path over there, you'll find the pond and some really terrific geese."

Fen's heart thundered in his chest. "You mean there are more?" he croaked, forgetting for the moment to be suave.

"Oh Lord, yes—outside and in. Come on. I'll take you to the pond. It's not often I get to show anyone who gives a damn."

"I find that hard to believe," Fen muttered.

Daria shrugged. "The family, except for Dad, are pretty bored with the whole thing," she said. "You should have heard the groans and moans when I applied to be a breeder of endangered animals, because obviously this was going to mean even more critters around the place. Not that they're particularly underfoot, except maybe out here." She laughed. "Lily almost lost her breakfast to a goose this morning. What a blast."

As she talked, Daria was setting a brisk pace across the lawn and down a long path that wound toward a grove of trees. Fen, followed closely by the llama and the young crane, strode in her footsteps, his mind swirling with questions and charged with anticipation.

The pond lay on the border between formal garden and woodland, and it swarmed with water birds. "The ducks are visitors," Daria said. "I don't bother to raise ducks myself since so many of them stop off here on their way north or south. Some even raise families at our place." She pointed to a brown duck with a yellow bill that sailed serenely on the shining surface of the water, a line of six plump ducklings paddling in her wake. Most of the ducks were brown, but Fen saw that in their brownness they varied enormously, their feathers shading from chocolate to buff to grey with delicate traceries of white. Some had a streak of blue under each wing. Along the shore three adult cranes walked with their deliberate grace through the green grass. "There's Suzy's mom," Daria said, "out there at the edge of the trees. She's got this ridiculous floating nest just to make my life difficult when I want to take an egg."

Fen stared across the pond at the great bird on its island of sticks and wondered how, even in the interest of producing more cranes, Daria could bring herself to disturb such proud tranquillity. Then he felt a tug on the hem of his bath sarong and looked down just as a shiny orange bill with a white ring around it was about to tug again. "White-fronted goose," Daria said. "Be careful or he'll have you buck naked in seconds, although buttons are his special love, and you don't seem to have any of those."

Fen thought if this beautiful creature really wanted his tedious garment, it was welcome to it, but firm admonishments about stripping in front of Terran females stayed his hand. There were, he saw, quite a lot of geese floating on the water in pairs or preening their feathers at the edge of the pond.

Daria sat down on a rock, and Fen crouched beside her on the grass. "I like to watch birds preen," she said, and there was something shy and appealing in her usually brisk voice.

"Who wouldn't?" he said.

"Oh, I don't know. It's something they do an awful lot of, and that's boring for most people."

"But there is immense variety in what they do," Fen said. He was watching a goose select one of its primary feathers, pull it firmly through its beak, and smooth it back into place. Another was fluffing the feathers on its breast with short, quick tugs.

Daria gave him a startled look. "You can see that, can you?"

"Of course."

"Well, most people can't. They just say, don't those birds ever stop poking at themselves, or something like that. Actually, it's super important for birds to keep their feathers in shape."

"What could be more obvious?" Fen said.

"You seem to know a lot about our animals," Daria said. "I should have thought with all the other stuff you had to learn—you know like, well obviously the language, and then I suppose social institutions and Earth history and all that kind of thing—there wouldn't have been time for zoology."

Fen paused, wondering how to put this as casually as possible. "Except for the language, no subject was given special emphasis. We had a certain amount of choice."

"And you chose animals?"

"Among other things," Fen said guardedly.

"Then maybe you can answer a question that's been bothering me," Daria said, and Fen silently prepared his defenses. He knew what the question was going to be. "Since you're so interested in our animals, I hope you'll be able to tell me all about yours. When we first started hearing about Chela and seeing all the pictures the explorers sent back, I sat glued to the screen, looking for animals. I was just six, but animals were already pretty much the only thing for me."

"And did you find them interesting?" Fen asked politely.

"There weren't any," Daria said, "any pictures, I mean. Just a lot of you folks in your nice, neat little towns and then massive doses of really pretty scenery and enough trees and flowers to drive a botanist around the bend, but nothing for me."

"How odd."

"Yes, wasn't it?"

"I suppose it was thought that humans would want to see intelligent life forms—namely us," Fen said carefully. "I really don't know. I also was very young when the first expeditions came. Then, too, our animals, except for a certain number of pests, live in the wild. Unlike you, we do not believe in locking them up," he finished in a burst of confidence. The Terran saying that the best defense is an offense was suddenly clear to him. What he was not prepared for was the fact that this remark would infuriate Daria.

"That's the stupidest thing I ever heard," she said, "or else your information is about a hundred and fifty years out of date. We don't lock animals up for our own amusement. How are we supposed to breed endangered species or make the studies that tell us how to save wild animals if we don't, as you so gracefully put it, lock a certain number of them up? I suppose on your wonderfully civilized, idyllic planet you don't need animal conservation programs."

"Correct. We do not," Fen said briefly.

Daria got up from her rock and started to walk away. "Well, lucky you," she said over her shoulder.

He saw that he had made a mistake—exactly the kind of mistake against which he had been warned—and now this intensely interesting person who seemed to know so much about animals was offended and walking away. "Daria, please don't be angry," he called after her. "Two beings from different planets are bound to have misunderstandings, but I am good at foreign concepts. It is one of the abilities for which I was selected."

Daria paused and looked back at him with a wry smile. "How amusing," she said. "Did you have some sort of test where they gave you twenty outrageous concepts and you answered on a scale of one to ten from 'I understand completely' to 'Sorry, I just can't swallow that'?"

"Something of the sort," Fen said.

"Quaint," Daria said, "but not in the end very helpful, I guess. Don't worry. I'm sure we'll get along fine, but right now I have a pile of stuff to do. Why don't you go in the kitchen—there's the door right there—and push a few food buttons? It looks as if Mom forgot about lunch, which is not surprising, since she never fixed lunch before in her life."

"I'm not hungry," Fen said to Daria's retreating back, and realized to his astonishment that this was true. Too much emotion, he thought, had disrupted his normal every-two-hour feeding pattern. He turned his attention once more to the water birds and almost immediately forgot about the girl. The human species was interesting as an example of parallel evolution and also, of course, because he was going to have to live with it. Fen was an intensely curious person, and there was much to be learned from a study of human beings—what they ate; how they mated and raised their young; their curious, seemingly dysfunctional customs, such as the locking of doors; and above all how they could be manipulated. He would not neglect his study of the human race, but the feathered panorama that stretched before his eyes was another thing entirely. He watched, hardly daring to breathe, as the cranes stalked through the long grass at the edge of the pond, stabbing at the ground with their sharp bills for hidden delicacies and pausing from time to time to survey their domain with round yellow eyes.

The goose that had made a bid for his sarong slid into the water, where it joined another goose, and the two sailed away together toward the rushes on the other side of the pond. A bonded pair, Fen thought. He had read that geese and cranes and indeed many other birds were faithful for life to their chosen partners, and he wondered whether he would be lucky enough to see them mating, defending their nests, and raising families.

Close to his left side Fen saw a solitary goose that crouched in the grass and stared out over the teeming surface of the water. Its feathers were dull and uncared for, and its lusterless eyes were sunken in its head. Sick or very old, Fen thought, and he felt a wave of anguish that such a beautiful creature could fail and die, even as he told himself sternly that all living things—Chelans, Terrans, and all the lovely creatures of Earth—were mortal. Still, he wondered if Daria knew about this goose. Perhaps she could do something. She was crossing the back of the garden again and stopped with an impatient toss of her head when Fen called out to her.

"I am anxious about this goose," Fen said when she had joined him by the pond. "It seems very sick, but perhaps you know. Please forgive me for meddling."

The girl's thin dark face softened as she looked down at

the bird. "She's not sick in any way that we can help, Fen, unless you know how to mend a broken heart. Her gander was shot last fall, and she's been this way ever since."

"Shot!" Fen cried. "What do you mean shot? It is not possible you still hunt animals."

"Well, we do," Daria said, "in a limited way, but this was worse. A man just drove up in his scooter and leaned out the window with a rifle. One bang and a beautiful young bird that might have lived twenty years with his mate was dead. There are people who get their kicks that way. Talk about sick. That's why I'm trying to keep the birds off the front lawn—another job for Peru, and he's pretty good at it, although sheepherding is more his game. I say, Fen, are you going to be okay?"

"No," Fen said in a muffled voice. "I don't think so." Waves of nausea were washing over him, and his skin had turned a horrible muddy grey. He put his head down and tried to turn his imagination off, but it was no use. He could see the proud gander on the green margin of the road, stopping perhaps to duck its head and preen the soft feathers of its breast, which in a moment would be shattered and dark with blood. He could see the light go out of its eyes and feel the terrible, senseless grief of the bereaved goose that would go on and on. Daria's voice came to him faintly as if from the end of a long tunnel dark with fear and horror.

"Please don't take it so hard," Daria said. She was kneeling beside him now and had stretched out a hand, then pulled it back, as if aware that he was beyond her reach. "I'm really sorry I told you. It's an awful story. I was a wreck when it happened, but you know he might have gotten torn up by a fox or run into a power line or a host of other things. He'd still be dead, and poor Lola would still be pining away. It happens, Fen."

He raised his head slowly and found that he was able to do so without fainting or throwing up. It seemed a major accomplishment. After a while he said, "I know about death and grief, Daria. What I did not know was that human beings were wanton killers."

"Well, live and learn," Daria said, with what Fen thought unsuitable flippancy. "You mean to tell me there's no dark side to the Chelan character?"

"We don't kill," Fen said flatly.

"None of you?"

"None of us."

"Well, bully for you," Daria said, and he realized, this time with something close to despair, that he had made her angry again, now when he truly needed solace and understanding.

"Daria," he said, "we are different, but we are not good. I will try to explain, but not now. Please forgive me."

She stared at him, and to his relief he saw the anger ebb away. "How about a ham sandwich?" Daria said.

Fen's stomach lurched again, and he shook his head. "Something else," he said. "Something happy-making."

Daria laughed and jumped to her feet. "Well, come then," she said. "We'll go to my room. I have several remedies for sadness there."

# eight

Giovanna Ferrante felt the single tear that rolled down her cheek but didn't care enough to brush it away. The young pathologist averted his gaze. He had been told that Giovanna sometimes cried at necropsies, and he had been told to ignore this embarrassing display. He was not to think that this very senior zoologist was sentimental, whatever the signs to the contrary. They were standing over the body of a female squirrel monkey, dead from a virus that had swept through a colony of thirty in the last two weeks. She was the last of their once large and robust breeding colony. She was also the last squirrel monkey in the world.

Giovanna reached out a gloved hand and briefly stroked the soft yellow fur down from the back to the pale cream of the belly. The head was capped with dark chocolate brown, the face white, the muzzle black. At the end of the long tail that drooped over the edge of the table was another tuft of dark fur. Giovanna lifted the tail and curled it around the small, dead animal, even though she knew that the young man standing so patiently across the table would soon reduce the last of the squirrel monkeys to a collection of organs and vials of fluids ready for the lab.

Sleep well, squirrel monkey, Giovanna thought, you and all your kind. We won't be watching your games anymore or helping you raise your tiny, rambunctious young or devising new habitats or congratulating each other on how well you are doing. You didn't do well enough. "This was a botch," she said to the young pathologist, her voice thick with anger and tears.

"You know we did everything we could," he said. "You know there wasn't any cure."

"Don't be stupid," Giovanna said. "I don't mean this case, this troop—all you good fellows staying up all night in the lab, all the keepers trying every trick they knew, going without sleep, watching their babies die one after the other, and having to come back in the morning for more of the same. And I don't blame the people in Zurich or San Diego or Rio. But there weren't enough squirrel monkeys, were there? And we didn't put them back in the wild, even though the habitats have been ready for ten years." The pathologist opened his mouth and closed it again as Giovanna swept on. "And don't tell me how much work it is to return a species to the wild or that there wasn't room in the zoos for more than four colonies. Don't you think I know all that?"

"Of course you do," he said. "I wasn't going to make any excuses for anybody. I was only going to remind you . . ."

"Don't," Giovanna said brutally. "If you were going to trot out a lot of success stories, please spare me that. And now get on with your work. Since we all know what she died of, it shouldn't take long, nor do I feel my presence is required."

"It's not, Giovanna," the young man said, adding unwisely, "Take a little time off, why don't you?"

"I have no time to take off," the director said from the door, "unless it is to stop and wonder which species will be next."

Sunlight flooded the rolling hills of Giovanna's domain, the vast extension of the Bronx Zoo where so many endangered animals lived and, she had to admit, often flourished, producing generations of healthy young. On her left the red-tiled roofs of the primate complex glowed in the strong light. Giovanna turned the other way. Just as there was no need for her to attend the necropsy, she could leave the fanatical cleaning and disinfection of the squirrel monkeys' empty house to her staff. Everyone was very good at his job, and the only thing that needed supervising was her own mind.

Wandering aimlessly, she found herself at last leaning on the wall to the large, dusty field where the herd of white rhinos snorted, stamped, and, against all odds, bred like rabbits, if that could be said of so unprolific an animal. A lot of it had been predictable, Giovanna thought—from the tragic drama of extinction in which the panda and the cheetah had been lost forever to the quiet demise of the kangaroo rat, the clown fish, and thousands of other tiny, uniquely fascinating animals. On the positive side, no one had been particularly amazed at the survival of all twenty-seven species of mongoose. But there had been surprises—many nasty, some quite wonderful, such as this walking fossil that had been so rare even before the environmental crash that no zoologist would have given a bent penny for its future. She smiled involuntarily as the newest addition to the rhino family set off at an awkward gallop, hit a patch of mud near their pool, and skidded on its little wrinkled rump. In a few years this infant would be on a plane to Africa, where five small but lusty herds were, for the first time in nearly a century, grazing their ancestral territory. Brilliant success stories, heartbreaking failures, and in between how many animals lived at varying degrees of risk?

Like the binturong and, to a lesser degree, the fennec fox. The image of Daria Wells sitting in the middle of her luxurious private zoo popped into Giovanna's mind and afforded her another slight smile. Daria was the youngest and by far the most ambitious of all the program's licensed breeders. She would make a fine zoologist one day, if she didn't burn herself out at the age of sixteen. Never had any childhood, Giovanna thought, and now she's missing her teens.

The old director shrugged. Giovanna hadn't had any childhood either. She had been in the tattered remains of the Amazonian rain forest with her parents trying to save the squirrel monkey and God only knew how many other embattled creatures—an appalling time that she recalled with more than a twinge of nostalgia. Another picture sprang up between her and the sunny field of grazing rhinos—a picture of torrential rain and hurricane-force wind screaming through the forest canopy as the entire research station disappeared in a wall of water. "Great days," Giovanna said to the baby rhino, which was leaning perilously over the edge of the moat to get a better look at her. "Thank God I was young." She had been ten at the time.

Daria's life seemed frivolous by comparison. But, of course, it wasn't. You had to judge your life by the times, and no one could deny that these times were better than those of Giovanna's youth, when every living creature, including the one who had caused it all, had seemed in imminent peril of extinction.

"Lucky Daria," Giovanna said, "and now she's got an alien, too." When she had been Daria's age, pretty much the only thought anyone had had about other planets was that it would be nice (if wholly impractical) to escape to one. Then, almost it seemed by accident, the galaxy drive had been discovered, and in a world exhausted by the rigors of reconstruction, the long grey years of labor had dropped away before the promise of the stars. "I must see the Chelan, *subito,* without delay," Giovanna cried. Invigorated by the thought of something so new and fascinating, she left the white rhinos and strode up the hill to her office, from which she could invade the privacy of the Wells house, with the important exception of Daria's room, efficiently and at high resolution.

# nine

Giovanna was to be frustrated in her search for Fen. Daria, exhausted by the alien's relentless curiosity about her animals, had dropped him off at the barn. "The last exhibit," Daria had said. "See what you make of it and tell me much later. I've got more work to do than you can possibly imagine."

The barn was very old. It had been built more than two hundred years ago at a time when architectural fancy had extended even to animal enclosures and was the only round barn Roger Wells had ever seen. In his long search for a place to build the house of his dreams, it had been the deciding factor. He had seen it all—the low white house with its upswept wings, the garden stretching down to the pond, and there, in the background, ancient, monolithic, looming between manicured lawn and shaggy wood, this wonderful barn. It was only much later, after the house had been built, that he had turned his mind to possible uses for his discovery. By that time Daria, his animal-obsessed daughter, had found that the barn was already occupied by, at a rough estimate, several thousand little brown bats.

The bats were a sort of zoological bonus, Daria had explained to Fen, since they had chosen the barn as a home without consulting her. "Bats are not everyone's cup of tea," she had said, "but they may well be yours. If they give you the creeps, just leave. It's all one to them."

It was more than an hour later that Fen, dizzy with happiness and covered with bat guano, emerged from the soft, rustling dark of the barn.

Lily, who had not seen the alien visitor since his arrival and who was trying to forget that he existed, came out of the house at the same moment. She was headed for a secluded spot in the garden and carried the full equipment of the twenty-first-century sunbather—towel, enormous hat, nearly black glasses, and number 51 sunscreen. The sight of Fen, now an intense shade of forest green splotched with patches of light grey, stopped her in her tracks. "No," Lily said. "No. I simply cannot cope with this."

If Fen heard this unfriendly remark, it failed to register. His reaction to the sight of his beautiful foster sister was simply that his cup ran over. "Lily, wait!" he cried, for she had turned as if to dart back into the house. "I have just had the most remarkable experience."

Lily stopped. "You've been in the barn," she said cautiously.

"Yes. Daria left me there alone because she had a lot to do. I sat down on a box and watched the bats. We have good night vision, and it's not really all that dark. After a while I could see them quite well, shuffling around on the rafters, stretching their wings, and then folding themselves up again into neat little packages. And I could hear them talking to each other, Lily, peeping sleepily in their tiny, high voices."

Fen had by this time lost command of the suave posture recommended by his mentors. This day had been too much. He was not only overexcited but desperately short of food and sleep. If Lily thought him less than cool, however, she gave no sign. "You're covered with bat shit," Lily observed.

Fen glanced down and saw that this was true. Given the intensity of his experience with the bats, he was not surprised to have arrived at such a state without being aware of it. On the other hand, Chelans are naturally clean, and Lily was clearly a fastidious person. It was unfortunate. "I'll jump in the pond and wash," he said.

"Don't put yourself out on my account."

"It will only take a moment, and then we can talk, unless..." Fen paused, struck by a new anxiety. "Do you think the birds will mind if I get in with them?"

"Oh God," Lily cried, clutching her head, "who knows? Who cares?"

"Perhaps I should ask Daria."

"I say just do it, unless you want to be conventional and have a shower in your own bathroom, but that would be dull."

"And time-consuming," Fen said, making a dash for the pond.

Lily watched, fascinated against her will, as the blotchy green figure waded into the shallow water, and even she was surprised at how little disturbance he caused among the waterfowl. "Too much to hope that he'll drown," Lily muttered. The pond had a deep end, but almost certainly not deep enough.

Sunbathing had lost its appeal, and Lily decided to retreat to the house while Fen was still immersed. This plan was thwarted by the appearance of her mother on the garden path and by the simultaneous purr of Roger's little electric car in the driveway. Gloria had changed into a becoming smock of the sort she imagined simple women donned to cook and clean. She had a wooden spoon in her hand and an expression of desperation on her face, which lightened at the sound of her husband's arrival. "Thank God, your father's here," she said. "I've been poring over Grandma Wells's cookbooks for hours, and lunch is still in its infancy."

"I think it's too late for lunch," Lily said.

"Well, dinner then. Whatever you call it, it's too much for me. Where is Fen?"

"In the duck pond. My idiot sister left him alone in the barn, and you can imagine what he's covered with. I urged him to take a shower, but he seemed to think a dip with the ducks would be swifter and more efficient."

"That was very inconsiderate of Daria."

"He loved it."

"Don't tell me we have another animal lover to contend with. Well, that will be nice for Daria. She's such a lonely child. Darling, you're just in the nick, although why you had to leave home at all today is beyond me."

Roger came through the arch of the carport and gave his wife a hug. "Why am I in the nick, and what are you doing with that spoon? You look like an ad for Mrs. Thingumy's homemade, reconstituted pancakes."

"I've been trying to cook a real meal for our guest. There he is, by the way, out in the duck pond. It seemed like the right thing to do, especially since he is extraordinarily interested in food. I thought if I just worked my way through a few things in your mother's cookbooks, it couldn't be that hard. Generations of really stupid women, after all, cooked three or four meals a day until quite recently. You're not listening."

Roger was staring over her head at the pond, where Fen floated on his back surrounded by ducks and geese. "How can I attend to anything but that amazing spectacle?" he said. "You forget that I haven't had all day to become accustomed to the sight of a large grey teenager from space."

"He's not grey," Lily said. "At least he wasn't when he went into the water. How odd."

"Well, he's grey now," Roger said. "What the hell is he doing in the pond?"

"Washing off some bat shit," Lily said.

"Sorry I asked. He seems to be emerging from the deep."

Fen had righted himself gently so as not to frighten the birds and found the cool, muddy bottom of the pond with his long toes. Now he began to wade slowly toward the shore. Despite the urgency with which he had taken the plunge, he had realized in an instant that a swim was exactly what he needed. The cool water dappled with sunlight, the lovely tranquillity of the waterfowl, the lacy pattern of leaves against the blue sky when he turned on his back, all had combined to restore the state of controlled calm to which he constantly aspired. His face was serene and his long body suitably grey.

"Welcome aboard," said Roger Wells, advancing to the edge of the pond with outstretched hand.

Fen shook the hand briskly as he had been taught to do but then did not let go. He felt a current of friendship and acceptance flowing from this slender figure—the father, the provider, the cook. "I am so happy," Fen said, "but I am dripping on your shoes. Please forgive me."

"Think nothing of it," Roger said. "These shoes are about to come off—usually my first act after a business trip—and shoe polishing is one of the few things the robot does well. How was the pond? I confess I never thought of it as a swimming hole."

"Delicious," Fen said. "I am refreshed but also very hungry. Would it be rude to ask if food will be forthcoming in the foreseeable future?"

Roger laughed. "In the foreseeable future, yes, but if I am to prepare a suitable welcome-to-Earth dinner, you'll have to be patient. Come to the kitchen, and we'll find something to hold you over. Should you put something on? The ladies seem to be averting their eyes."

Fen retrieved the bath sarong from the edge of the pool and wound it around his waist. "It is hard for me to remember all of your taboos when everything else is so interesting," he said as they walked back to the house.

"Of course it is," Roger said. "Don't give it another thought. Lily will survive, and my wife is just pretending, aren't you, my love?"

"You can look now," Gloria told her daughter. "He is clothed, if that's the word for it. Take poor Fen to the kitchen, Roger, and give him something to eat. I've been a dismal failure in that department."

With the obvious exception of Daria's room, the kitchen would become Fen's favorite place in the house. Since Chelans ate in automated dining halls, he was unaccustomed to the idea of a room devoted to the actual making of food, and indeed to many Terrans the Wells kitchen would have seemed strange. Roger, who spent his professional life on the advance edge of modern design, liked to cook the old-fashioned way—up to his elbows in primary ingredients, the gooier the better. The food slots were a concession to the fact that he was often away from home. Without them the rest of the family might have starved.

Gloria had already laid out a number of rather random ingredients, most of which Roger now began to stow away, and the kitchen seemed to Fen's starved senses to be a wonderland of smells and tastes. Moving fast, he was able to sample baking soda, lemon peel, butter, and raw egg before Roger whisked them out of sight.

"I think she was planning to make a cake," Roger muttered. "What a hope."

"And you are not going to make a cake?" Fen asked, trying to keep the disappointment out of his voice and failing dismally.

"You want a cake?"

"Very much, if possible."

"What kind?"

"How do I know?" Fen said. "Except for an excellent sandwich provided upon my arrival here and the delicious snacks on the train, my knowledge of your cuisine is entirely academic."

Suppressing a shudder at the thought of what had already passed over these virgin taste buds, Roger gazed thoughtfully at his victim. "Are you allergic to any of our food so far as you know?" he asked.

"We are allergic to nothing," Fen said. "Exhaustive tests were run, which was all very tedious since it was done by injection rather than by sampling the actual foods."

"I suppose it would have been impractical to bring samples of even our commonest foods back to Chela for you to try," Roger said. "Good Lord, we must be talking about several million items. I also doubt that your people were able to test you for every possible chemical combination. You'd be as full of holes as a pincushion."

"Our technology is very advanced," Fen said. "But let's not talk about that."

Roger reached into a cupboard and produced a large bar

of semisweet chocolate. "Right. Back to basics," he said. "Here is a common cake ingredient with almost universal appeal. See what you think. It's called chocolate, and I only have the one, so you may eat exactly one third, not an ounce more or we'll have to have a different kind of cake."

Fen ate the chocolate slowly, as he felt appropriate to one making an important decision. By the time he had finished his alloted share, he was pink from head to foot and experiencing a kind of giddy euphoria much like that which had swept over him in the early days of his friendship with Filya.

Roger, never one to let manners stand in the way of curiosity, stared at his guest. Although it was possible that glowing yellow eyes in a smiling pink face signified rage or despair, it seemed safe to conclude that chocolate had met with approval. "Do you always turn pink when you are pleased?" he asked.

"Always," Fen said. He was feeling so happy, so physically and mentally restored, that it seemed unnecessary either to apologize for or to explain his color change.

"How odd," Roger said, "because we do, too, though to a much more limited extent. And we have other metaphors that have absolutely no correspondence with reality. Do you, for example, turn green with envy?"

Fen shook his head. "Chrome yellow. Green is for a more serious kind of joy than that produced by food or sex or other creature comforts."

"And this pleasant but decidedly neutral grey?"

"A cloak," Fen said, wondering as he spoke why he was willing to talk of such intimate matters with someone he had only just met. "An absence of color denotes an absence of emotion. Of course, there can be an element of deception here."

"Meaning that a grey Chelan is not necessarily feeling grey."

"We can control it up to a point. The surge of hormones that triggers the expanding and contracting of the color cells beneath our skins can be quenched by an act of will. Some are better at this than others, and it is a discipline that grows with age. Even for a young person, I am considered rather a failure at color control." Fen smiled ruefully. "Had I not been so exceptionally intelligent and strong willed, this would have prevented my selection for the exchange program."

"Strange," Roger said. "I should have thought that openness would have been valued in an emissary, but you're suggesting that grey was the color of choice in the selection process. Why?"

"You shouldn't confuse grey with dismal or unfriendly," Fen said. "A grey Chelan can be just as sociable as, for example, a pink one. It's just that he or she isn't giving anything important away."

"And do you people have a lot to hide?"

"No more than you, I should think." With a feeling that he had been led unawares into deep waters, Fen turned away from the friendly but alarmingly intelligent brown eyes of his foster father and began to wander around the kitchen. "Shouldn't you be doing something with the rest of that chocolate?" he said.

"I should, and I will. Unfortunately, cooking is only the second passion of my life. Prying information out of interesting people is my first." Roger turned to study the electronic display on the refrigerator door, which provided a complete list of what was inside, including date of purchase, shelf location, and state of freshness. Then he went to work with a swiftness born of long practice and passionate enthusiasm.

Fen watched enthralled as ingredients were pulled from the refrigerator and cupboard shelves, sorted into bowls, and fed into the food processor. "What a quaint machine," he said as the blades whirred to a halt, leaving a wonderful-looking light brown batter in the bowl.

"Quaint?" Roger said. "I understood it was top of the line. Get this, for example. You don't have to set any dials or poke any buttons to tell it what it's working with. It senses the ingredients, whether they're hard or soft, fibrous or smooth. All you have to do is tell it what you want done with them."

Fen nodded but was clearly unimpressed. "I know nothing of food production," he said. "I merely feel that this is like a machine we might have used about two hundred years ago."

"Well, so you're ahead of us. It would be positively disquieting if our two planets turned out to have the same technology at the same stage of development. Of course, we would be much farther ahead except for the crash, but ahead in what, I often ask myself. We learned to do the important things, and we learned them fast."

"The crash?"

"The environmental crash. You must have learned about that."

"We learned," Fen said, and something in his voice made Roger look up from pouring the cake batter into the pans. The alien had turned slate grey, and his yellow eyes burned in their cavernous sockets. "We learned," he said again, "but it was hard for us to understand how such a catastrophe could have happened so suddenly or how so intelligent a race could have failed to see it coming."

"We often wonder that ourselves," Roger said cheerfully, "and so far nobody has a really satisfactory explanation. It was as if one minute we were standing around with our thumbs up our asses, discussing what to do about global warming, and the next minute our heads were underwater, among other unpleasant things. Of course, it wasn't quite that fast; it took about ten years to reach its peak of awfulness—considerably less than a minute in the usual course of climate change."

"You speak very lightly of a terrible event," Fen said.

"Not really, but look: number one, this was seventy years ago, so I wasn't even born, and two, we are proud of having saved ourselves from what was a very near thing."

"And what of the ones that were not saved?"

Roger took the full cake pans carefully from the table and slid them into the oven, then turned to face his fierce young interlocutor. "You may find this a brutal thing to say, but there were two good things to come out of this disaster: we learned how to live so that, if we persevere in our new ways, it won't happen again, and we drastically reduced world population. Grim but true. I count myself lucky that I was not around to witness the carnage."

Fen swayed. The kitchen seemed to be tilting under his feet, and his stomach lurched. "I was thinking of the animals," he said in a faint voice.

"Whoa. Hang on. Here's a chair." Roger shoved a kitchen chair against Fen's knees and stood gazing down at him anxiously. "You were thinking of the animals, not of the human population," he said. "You sound like Daria, not that there's anything wrong with that. But most people, when they look back on the crash, think of all the human beings who drowned or died in epidemics or simply killed each other off in the endless little wars that raged among starving and terrified people."

Fen raised his head. "Countless wonderful animal species were lost and will never be seen again, here or anywhere else in the universe," he said.

Roger pulled a box of crackers from a shelf and thrust it at Fen, who regarded it with distaste. "I should have given you something else to eat," he said. "Chocolate does that sometimes, and of course you're not used to it. Way up, then way, way down. Talk about crashes. Please eat a few of these boring things, and then, perhaps, you should get some rest."

"I'm all right," Fen said stubbornly. "I want to talk."

"Talk to Daria, or better yet to Giovanna Ferrante at the Hudson Valley Ark. Giovanna is seventy-six and has been working to save the animal victims of the crash since she was knee-high to a salamander. There probably isn't anything she can't tell you, and since you seem to care so much, I guarantee she'll be delighted to talk. Meanwhile, eat some crackers. If you pass out, I doubt I could get you into bed."

"You would find me surprisingly light," Fen said, "but I see your point." He sampled a cracker and then another. Quite soon the box was empty, and his color had improved. "Sleep is, in fact, not such a bad idea," he conceded, getting rather shakily to his feet. "Don't let me miss dinner."

"You can count on me," said Roger Wells, watching with relief as the strange, fragile figure of his young visitor made its unsteady way through the kitchen door.

# ten

The light of late afternoon poured through the long window by Fen's bed, while on the lawn ducks squabbled, cranes and geese wandered through the grass, and the tall llama, Peru, grazed with a watchful brown eye on the throng that was in his charge.

Fen had supposed that he would dream of this astonishing day—of snakes and tamarins, turtles and foxes, storks, mongooses, binturongs, and bats. Instead he dreamed of home.

At first he was in his mother's garden. It was hot, but a breeze blew from the lake and stirred the long tendrils of the loblo tree that shaded the vines and their heavy amber fruit. A good year, Fen thought, with many fewer insects than the year before. He reached out absently and decapitated a fat catch-claw that had buried its sharp proboscis in one of the fruits. To his annoyance the thing immediately grew another head, and then he saw that he had been wrong; the vines were crawling with catch-claws and with the smaller but more vicious brown ratchet bugs. "I'm really tired of this," Fen said to the insects. "I'm going away now. Somebody else will have to pinch off your heads."

He could hear the catch-claws and ratchets laughing as he turned to go. It was an evil, crackling sound like fire moving through dry brush, and Fen was suddenly terrified. He began to run through what had become a sea of insects that rose around his ankles and pulled him back. The buzzing, chittering horde grew higher and thicker with every step, and he knew that soon it would drag him down. I must reach the river, Fen thought, but the river was impossibly far away, and now he remembered that it had dried up a year ago. He gave a great strangled cry for help, at which the insects swirled up in a cloud before his eyes, and he fell.

He woke under a blanket of fog on the bank of the river he had thought was dead and lay for a time with his eyes closed listening to its voice. It seemed enough to lie still, knowing that the insects were gone and the river was here by his side, almost close enough to touch. A splash, followed by a contented grunting sound, caused him to open his eyes and then to sit up staring into the mist. At first he could see nothing, but gradually he became aware of movement on the opposite bank. Tall shapes moved through the fog, and then a light breeze thinned the veil before his eyes, and he gave a low cry of fear and joy, for there across the quiet water, the animals of Chela were coming down to drink.

A tall farlin came first. Its tightly curled grey coat made it almost invisible against the fog, but light caught the white enamel on its single horn as it bent to drink, and green eyes flashed as it raised its head. Now a silver kisiner slipped almost between the farlin's legs and slid down the muddy bank. Slender but deadly, its double row of needle teeth flashed for a moment as it lifted a dripping muzzle and yawned. Next came the delicate grassland runners with subtle zigzag patterns of rust and blue camouflaging their tawny coats, and tikitin, a golden fuzz ball with long ears lopped over its small pink eyes, hopping to the water on ridiculously thin hind legs. On and on they came—large and small, swift and slow, colorful and dull, predator and prey—in a seemingly endless parade. A great rustling in the branches announced the arrival of coplana, the Chelans' nearest relative. A magnificent female with long rust-colored fur tipped with electric blue walked erectly down the bank and dipped a folded leaf into the water. A tiny infant clung to the thick crest of hair on the top of her head.

Dreaming, Fen held his breath and found, to his surprise, that it was not necessary to breathe. He trailed a hand in the water and felt it brushed by a multitude of swimming forms, while overhead the sky was full of beating wings. Because he dreamed, he was not disturbed by the presence of predator and prey drinking together at the same watering place, nor by the mingling of species from widely separated habitats. He felt only wonder and an enormous gratitude that he should be given the sight of so many animals.

Something rustled and chirped on his side of the river, and Fen's heart jumped in his chest. A small creature, not much larger than Filya's cat, had appeared on a rock almost within his reach. It had its back to him and seemed to be looking out over the river at its fellow creatures.

"Greetings, mir-akona," Fen whispered. Large ears fringed with feathery white hairs rotated toward the sound of his voice and back again, and a shiver ran down the beautifully articulated spine, causing the thin coat of dark blue fur to ripple from neck to tail. "I will not harm you," Fen began, but the words caught in his throat. Slowly the mir-akona turned its head and gazed at him with huge grey eyes. "I will not!" Fen cried, and suddenly the animals were gone and he was lying on stony ground by a dry watercourse, racked with a terrible, nameless grief.

It was growing dark when Fen opened his eyes on the real world of Earth, and he lay for a while looking out at the trees against the evening sky, hearing the soft sounds birds make before they sleep, and enjoying the immense relief of one who finds that the sorrow and terror so recently experienced were, after all, only a dream.

A small but insistent signal emanating from under his pillow brought him fully awake. Filya was calling, and to judge by her expression when he stretched his monitor enough so that he could see it, she had been calling for some time. "Napping is fine," Filya said. "God knows we all need to nap. But we're also supposed to wake easily and be instantly alert to outside stimuli."

Fen blinked at the wrathful face of his future bride and wondered that he wasn't happier to see her. An hour ago, if he had not been so exhausted, he would have been eager to recount the astounding events of the afternoon. Now it seemed as if there was too much to tell and all of it too fraught with complicated and devastating emotions. He needed a really wise and sympathetic listener and thought with longing of U-Bandor, his mentor on Chela. "Please, Filya, my love," he said, "I have had a wonderful but also very trying day and just now a really terrifying dream."

Her face softened. "I saw that you dreamed, and at first I was envious because you looked so happy, but it had a bad end, didn't it? You should tell me about it."

I should, Fen thought, but I can't, at least not now, though Filya would understand, as would even the most insensitive Chelan. "I'd rather tell you about my animals," he said.

The soft blue tuft over Filya's left eye twitched quizzically. "Animals, plural?" she said. "And you were afraid there wasn't even one. I won't say I told you so. What have you got?"

"You're not going to believe this."

"Try me."

Before Fen finished his tale, delicious smells were finding their way under his door so that he was torn between the pleasure of the recitation and the desire to go begging for an appetizer. Filya, however, was not about to let him go. She had run through every color of the spectrum while he talked, settling at last into an intense shade of green tinged with gold. Fen read this as passionate, but not entirely selfless, joy. He could hardly blame her for feeling jealous, but her first words when she recovered the power of speech came as a surprise. "Fen," she cried, "what in all the universe are we going to do with this bonanza?"

His brain felt numb, probably from lack of food. "Do with what?" he said.

"I can't believe you could be so thick," Filya said. "There you are with representatives of what—fifteen or twenty animal species?—right within your grasp, and you say, 'Do with what?' We must acquire them, Fen. What could be more obvious? Why are we here?"

"To study animals," he said. "Nothing was said about abducting them."

"But much was implied."

"Filya, use your head," Fen shouted. "We couldn't abduct a field mouse, much less a full-grown llama. What kind of miraculous sleight of hand did you have in mind?"

Filya looked chastened but determined. "All I know is that we have to think of something," she said, "and you, my friend, must think the hardest of all."

# eleven

After a meal that far exceeded his most lavish dreams, Fen was puzzled by the swift dispersal of the family. On the rare occasions that so elaborate a banquet was prepared on Chela, the diners lingered long and lovingly at table, talking of this and that and in particular of the pleasures of the meal just eaten and of others fondly remembered. This was not only considered polite; it was also part of the fun.

Lily, to Fen's distress, took off without even tasting the tall brown cake with its lustrous swirls of chocolate frosting. "Not for me, thanks," she said, and no one else seemed surprised or offended.

"She worries about getting fat," Tim said after a look at Fen's astonished face. This was an explanation of sorts, since he had seen fat people from the window of the train, without realizing that fatness might be considered either bad or avoidable.

Daria and Tim both did full justice to the cake, which Tim pronounced to be "far out" before bolting from the table. Daria went so far as to give her father a quick hug. "Super meal, Dad," she said, and then she was gone.

Roger, who seemed contented with the minimal praise of his family, went off to the kitchen to supervise Esfor. Only Gloria appeared to be in no hurry to depart. "They're all so busy," she said. "I enjoyed an indolent youth and wonder if it isn't better that way, but they seem to thrive on activity."

"What are they busy at?" Fen asked. "Lily and Tim, that is. It is easy to see what occupies Daria."

"Daria is certainly special," Gloria said with a sigh. "Who would have thought that I would give birth to a zoologist, much less give a home to a zoo? But it makes her happy, and this is what mothers are supposed to want. Lily hopes to become a clothes designer. You must ask her to show you some of her designs on the computer, if that sort of thing interests you."

"Hardly at all," Fen confessed, "although I would pretend to please Lily. She doesn't seem to like me very much."

"Lily is very conventional, but the way to her heart is definitely through her designs. Perhaps she will make something for you to wear to school. I can't imagine what we might buy that wouldn't look awful, and she might find it a challenge."

"I had hoped the issue of clothes would just go away after a while," Fen said. "After all, I am an alien, and if you covered me up from chin to toes, I still wouldn't look like one of you."

Gloria laughed. "I see your point," she said, "and we can let the whole thing slide a while. You only arrived this morning and have a lot of new ideas to get used to. Just remember that the thing about clothes in this society is that they ease transitions and help people to concentrate on the important things about new acquaintances, like whether they're funny and smart or dumb and boring. We still have minds that go straight for the genitals, Fen, so if one of us meets someone wearing nothing but a little rag around his middle, the first question that will spring to mind is, What's underneath? Whereas if you're wearing a tunic and pants, that might be the third or fourth thing to pop into a person's head."

"I find that utterly bizarre but will bear it in mind," Fen said. "Now what about Tim?"

"Don't let Tim fool you. He's not such a lightweight as he makes himself out to be. Tim writes music, if *writes* is the word for what he does and *music* is the word for the outcome. You can hear it now, as a matter of fact, which means either he's turned it up past what we allow or his door is open a crack. We spent a fortune soundproofing his room, but it's not always one hundred percent successful."

When Gloria stopped talking, Fen became aware of a thin wailing sound in the extreme upper register, which was punctuated by periodic thumps and crashes. It was interesting and reminded him, if only very slightly, of certain Chelan tunes. "I am fond of music," he said. "Do you think I could enter his room and ask to hear more?"

"I think you would be more than welcome," Gloria said, "unless he's very busy indeed, and then he wouldn't even notice you were there. Tim is an amiable soul; he won't bite your head off. But don't try to knock. Just walk right in, and close the door tightly for my sake."

Greatly intrigued, Fen followed the sounds down the hall to the door that was unmistakably Tim's. It was slightly ajar. He slipped inside and closed it softly behind him.

Tim sat with his back to the door, which gave Fen a chance to study the room. This he did with a mixture of bewilderment and delight. The electronic marvels of his own civilization were awesome but unobtrusive and not something to which he ever gave much thought. Therefore this jungle of snaking wires, winking lights, and pulsing tubes was enchanting, like a play park at night when all the big games have been turned on and the smallest Chelan children run from one to the other pulling this and pushing that just to see what will happen next.

After listening and watching for a few minutes, Fen concluded that the high wailing sound was indeed electronic in origin and resulted from the depression of various keys on an enormous triple keyboard, while the thumps and crashes issued from a wondrous collection of antique percussion instruments. Tim sat in a veritable forest of snare drums and timpani, cymbals and gongs, bongos and bells, to mention only a few of the more identifiable items.

While one hand stroked the keyboard, the other reached out to whack an ancient drum.

Moving cautiously, Fen located a stool near the door and perched where he could see and hear. Not that hearing was any problem. The ceiling was honeycombed with amplifiers, and at times the volume rose to fearsome heights. That was all right with Fen, whose ears were equipped with a small shutter mechanism that opened and closed automatically. After what seemed rather a long time, the keyboard sounds faded away, and, turning from the console, Tim leaned over a small skin-covered drum. He was smiling broadly at Fen, who had the impression that his presence was no surprise. Long fingers danced and rapped, and the little drum spoke in its many voices. Then it, too, fell silent.

Tim got up and stretched and pushed his lavender hair out of his eyes. "Thanks for coming to the concert," he said.

"Do you have trouble getting an audience?"

"Believe it, my friend. Sometimes I confess to leaving the door open just the merest crack to give myself the feeling that there's someone out there listening, however reluctantly."

"Like tonight."

"Did I leave the door open tonight?"

Fen nodded solemnly. "Just a crack."

Tim laughed. "Yeah. Well, I had to know, you know? Whether someone from another planet might dig my stuff? Now, of course, I hate to ask."

"Dig?" Fen said. "As in excavate it from underground?"

"Hell, I'm sorry. Mom's right. I've got to cut this out. Dig is old music talk, and I mean really old, like a hundred years old. Nobody says it anymore, and you wouldn't be the only one not to get it. It means appreciate in a big way—not just like, but understand and relate to and well just . . ."

"Dig," Fen said. "Dig would be going too far, if it means understand. Who can understand the music of another race upon first hearing? But I do think it rather beautiful."

Tim turned almost as pink as a feeding Chelan and ducked his head. "That gives you an edge on the rest of the world," he said. "I wonder what you see in it, or would that be asking too much?"

"It would."

"Quite right," Tim said. "I can't describe it myself, but it gets better and better, you know, and it's pretty much all I want to do."

"Your equipment is astonishing," Fen said.

"All antique, every stick, every wire, every blinking little light," Tim said proudly.

"Really? Not just the drums and so on?"

"Lord, no, man. Electronics like this have been gone from the world for at least a century. I've bought the bits and pieces at barn sales and gone through absolute middens of old junk. It's one gigantic original instrument. Lucky I have a fairly well-off pa. The electronic stuff doesn't cost much, but old drums and gongs and whatnot, some of them from cultures that don't even exist anymore . . . well, you can imagine."

"I can try." The money economy of Earth was puzzling

to Fen but not very interesting. His new family, however, surpassed his highest hopes.

The exchange students had been warned to expect rather little of their human hosts, who were described as almost certainly kind and hospitable but not much more. "They will be anxious to please you," the instructors said, "and it should be easy to get them to take you to where the animals are." Thinking of this, Fen smiled to himself. No field trips to see animals would be required from this household, and although only one or two of its members seemed to care for animals, the others were fascinating in their own ways. He wondered whether he had been lucky or this family was typical and his instructors mistaken.

"Are there many families like this one?" Fen asked.

"Like in what way? You mean everybody zeroed in on a different career and totally oblivious of everyone else and forty-odd wild beasties in the youngest sibling's bedroom? Not a chance, old man. If you mean a mom and pop and three kids, even that is a bit outside the norm. It's because Lily and I are twins. Mom decided she could count us as one offspring, which is typical of the way she thinks—not muddled precisely, just creative to the point of lunacy, but that's part of her charm. You know couples are only allowed to have two children?"

Fen nodded. "It seems odd to us because our planet is underpopulated," he said. "But, yes, we know of this rule, and I suppose it makes sense if you really have too many people."

"Way too many. Even now after we killed off a whole

lot of them back in the twenties. How come you have so few?"

Fen looked down at his hands, which were darkening rapidly, as was the rest of him, from the soft, muted rose that was the aftermath of dinner. "We had a plague," he mumbled, "or something, about five hundred of your years ago. There were few Chelans left when it was over."

"Hey, sorry I asked," Tim said hastily. "Is it one of those things no Chelan likes to talk about? If so, consider it unmentioned."

"Why should I mind? It was all so long ago." Fen's color was improving, and he congratulated himself on this evidence of mind over matter. "I don't know much about it anyway," he went on. "History bores me."

"Really? I find it riveting—at least late-twentieth-century history, which is where all my stuff comes from. But to each his own. What interests you?"

"Animals, food, music—in that order, I fear."

"You've come to the right place," said Tim. "I wish I could share your enthusiasm for fur and feather. It would make this a much nicer place to live, though to be fair, except for the outdoor birds and llamas, Daria keeps the creatures out of our hair. What do you see in them anyway?"

"What do I see in what? That's like asking what you see in B-flat."

"It's what? Oh, I see." Tim frowned. "Well, what do you see, for example, in a bat—sorry, in one of Daria's bats, the kind she keeps in the barn?"

"I see..." Fen closed his eyes for a moment, the better to summon up and communicate in what was, after all, still a foreign language, the intense essence of batness to this seemingly receptive Terran. "I see a near-perfect predator, wrapped in the softest fur and borne on the most elegant of wings. I see tiny warm bodies hanging by their toes with their babies cradled under the dark rafters, or swooping forth in the dusk to hunt with the echo of their voices. All this is a miracle to me and leaves me breathless with excitement. I suppose it must be the same for Daria, although she seems much more practical and prosaic than I."

"She'd better be," Tim said, "or she'd never get anything done."

Fen saw that he had failed to communicate what he felt about bats and perhaps even made a fool of himself. But, no, Tim's gaze was benign, if a little distracted. In fact, he might be said to be looking straight through his visitor. "Excuse me just a mo, old man," said Tim, and wheeled around into the thicket of his instruments. A deep, throbbing sound crept from one of the speakers above Fen's head to be joined by a series of sharp, whistling shrieks.

The hall was empty when Fen slipped away and silent once he had closed the door. He stood for a moment, feeling the strange house around him, so still yet he believed so full of purposeful activity, and suddenly he was once again on the verge of exhaustion. I'll sleep now, he thought, and then perhaps go into the garden late at night or visit Daria in her room.

# twelve

By the time Fen had gone to his room to sleep, Giovanna, who had been hoping for just such an opportunity to observe him, was otherwise engaged. A shipment of eleven short-clawed Malaysian otters had arrived from Philadelphia, which was experiencing a sort of otter glut. This was fine with Giovanna, who had long coveted a collection of these jolly little mustelids. The enclosure, a generous piece of riverbank with a cozy sleeping hut, was ready, or so everyone thought. It was just that the otters were a day early and the workman who was responsible for giving the fence a final check was sick.

Otters sometimes have adjustment problems, but the ones from Philadelphia, perhaps because they were an extended family, lost no time in making a joyful inspection of their new home and finding a weak spot in the fence.

Soon there seemed to be otters everywhere. The two that had managed to open one of the refrigerators in the canid complex and were ransacking it (unsuccessfully) for fish were the first to be captured. The adolescent pup that had fallen asleep in the back seat of Giovanna's car was the last. It was getting dark, and the people who were fixing the fence began to doubt that they could make it really otter-tight until morning, so they dumped the whole squirming, biting, screeching lot of them into the empty monkey cage with several buckets of fish and enough old blankets to bed them down.

Giovanna was feeling her age by the time the last otter was tucked in. She left the equally exhausted group of young keepers and grounds people drooping in the cafeteria and trudged home through the woods.

The director's house had been a Victorian gamekeeper's cottage, which amused Giovanna, who devoted her life to the preservation of animals for rather different purposes. It was considered quaint by those who did not have to live in it and a dark, cramped monstrosity by most of those who did. Giovanna, however, enjoyed the denlike qualities of her house, as well as its location, deep in the thickly wooded wolf habitat that occupied the northeast quadrant of the Ark. Her relationship with the wolves, who had their own den under a rock outcropping not far from the cottage, was excellent, and she felt comfortably insulated from the rest of the world.

Closing the door with a sigh of relief, she went to the kitchen and opened a bottle of mediocre red wine—mediocre because it wasn't going to have much time to breathe, red because there was a pan of leftover lasagna in the refrigerator that would do for supper. Giovanna's parents, who had lived most of their lives in appalling discomfort, had not neglected to instill in their daughter certain values, among them the importance of wine with the final meal of the day. She put the lasagna in the oven, poured a glass of wine, and went to sit in her favorite chair. The fact that it was also the favorite chair of an eighteen-foot python was only a momentary inconvenience. *"Scusa, caro,"* Giovanna said, and stood patiently while the enormous reptile slid slowly to the floor. She was fond of snakes, which was fortunate since her husband, currently tagging anacondas in Venezuela, was a herpetologist, and half a dozen splendid specimens shared the cottage. They were ideal pets for a busy person since they didn't need to eat very often, nor did they pine for company. They were beautiful, interesting, and emotionally undemanding.

It was not until Giovanna was settled in her chair that she remembered the alien and how eager she had been to meet him earlier in the day. Forgetting the lasagna but hanging on to her wine, Giovanna negotiated the narrow, snake-haunted stairs to her room. She had a powerful little computer up there and an old-fashioned red telephone that was only supposed to ring in the most dire emergencies. "I'll just take a peek before supper," Giovanna said to the boa that occupied her bed. "He's probably asleep, *poveretto.* To journey from another planet and end up in the house of Wells. The spirit quails at the thought."

The large, high-resolution screen on Giovanna's bedroom wall showed, as she had thought it would, a very soundly sleeping alien. Fen was a deep rosy lavender, the color of contented sleep, from head to foot. He was also uncovered and unclothed—the answer to a snooping zoologist's prayer.

Knowing that there would be many opportunities to observe a creature who was the long-term guest of her protégée, Giovanna took no notes. Instead she simply gazed with amazement and delight. It was like the old days, she thought, when you stalked a rare animal for days, weeks, sometimes months, and then suddenly came to the edge of a clearing, and there it was, sleeping or grooming its fur or eating or staring disconcertingly into the thick vegetation you had thought so concealing. Such moments made the hard life of a field zoologist worthwhile. Now here she was, pretty much retired from tramping through the jungle, sitting in a soft chair and staring at a creature from another planet. A humanoid creature, Giovanna reminded herself, a creature who had mastered at least one of her languages and to whom she would therefore be able to talk. It was really remarkable how humanoid he was. She recalled a thousand arguments with other scientists on the question, If we ever find another sentient species in the universe, what will it be like? Beyond agreeing that it would need something like hands for tool using, there had been little consensus. It was a very conservative school of thought which maintained that the primate/human body plan was a good one and would probably be reproduced by evolution on any planet that was otherwise similar to Earth.

Giovanna examined Fen from the tips of his extraordinarily long toes to the shock of feathery black hair on the top of his head, and then her eyes came back to rest on the middle of his chest and the only thing he wore besides his beautiful lavender skin.

"A tooth," Giovanna said out loud, "an animal tooth mounted in gold." Aware that there was no reason to expect any correspondence between the tooth of a Chelan animal and that of anything on Earth, she nevertheless started flipping through her mental file of teeth, finding it a bit like this and a bit like that but not exactly like anything. She increased the magnification of the amulet until it was the only thing on the screen. At the same moment a long-fingered hand slid into view and covered it up. Giovanna's fingers trembled on the control as she pulled back. The alien was awake, and, like the animal in the clearing, he was staring straight into her eyes. As he stared, his skin began to darken and lose color until it was a uniform slate grey, which made his amber eyes all the more disturbing.

It was hard to know what to say. Belatedly, Giovanna realized what Daria could have told her—that looking in on a sleeping alien visitor was not quite the same as observing a leopard from a blind.

"Please excuse this intrusion," Giovanna said.

The stranger swung his feet to the floor and stood up, at the same time winding a meager piece of cloth around his waist. "Can you think of one good reason why I should?" he said.

Giovanna produced the smile that in former days had brought the chiefs of foundations to their knees. "Not just at the moment," she said, "but I am determined to try."

The haughty stare wavered, and she saw that he was looking past her at something in the background. "That is a truly enormous and beautiful snake," Fen said.

Glancing over her shoulder at the boa, which had picked this moment to stir languidly on the bed, Giovanna reflected on how often animals came to the rescue when people were at a loss for words. "Isn't he?" she said. "Has a lovely disposition, too. Are you fond of snakes?"

"Hugely. My friend Daria, whose house this is, has three wonderful snakes, but they are much smaller than yours."

"I know," Giovanna said. "I gave them to her. Perhaps I should introduce myself. I am Giovanna Ferrante, and I am a zoologist, which is the only excuse I can offer for invading your privacy. Daria promised that we should meet, but I am hopelessly curious and could not wait for a proper introduction."

The effect of this announcement was startling. At first seeming to blush under his grey skin, Fen gradually turned a rich, deep rose all over and began to stammer. "I am honored. Your name is known to my people. Daria did not tell me that she knew so distinguished a scientist. Please forgive my former rudeness. Your interest is natural." He sputtered to a stop, and Giovanna hastened to fill the gap in the conversation.

"Natural perhaps," she said, "but still dreadful manners.

Are your people especially interested in zoology?"

This question elicited another bewildering response. "No more than anything else," the young alien said airily. "But you are famous in the field. We were made to learn the names of many intellectual leaders."

"I couldn't help noticing," Giovanna continued, "that you wear an animal tooth around your neck. There are still a few members of forest-dwelling tribes on Earth who do the same, but they are much less sophisticated than you."

"It's not a tooth," Fen said quickly. "What a bizarre idea. It's just a little symbolic thing for the exchange students to wear, sort of like a . . ." He searched his mind for some Terran analogy. "Like one of your class rings," he finished triumphantly. "Each of us got one before we left, which was silly, since jewelry is not something we care about."

"Have you looked at this trinket at all closely?"

"Of course. Archival-grade plastic mounted in what I fear is only the thinnest of gold plate. Why it was made to look like a tooth is hard to imagine."

Giovanna sighed. "Whimsy. There's no accounting for whimsy, is there? Still, being an incorrigibly curious old nuisance, I would like to examine it when we meet face to face."

"Why not?" Fen said, but he was trembling, and his color had darkened dramatically, a reaction Giovanna decided to ignore.

"You must beg Daria to bring you here in person," she

said. "Whether you are interested in zoology or not, you will find this place fascinating. Here we breed a hundred different species of endangered animals by the most advanced methods. I will give you the grand tour, and in return you will answer a thousand questions about the animals of your planet. How does that sound?"

"It sounds wonderful," Fen said rather faintly. "But please do not expect great things from me. I really know very little about Chelan animals. You will have to forgive me."

"I think I have been not only rude but cruel to wake you in the middle of the night when you are understandably exhausted," Giovanna said. "It is I who should be forgiven. Please go back to sleep. We will talk again soon."

It seemed to Giovanna that even as the image faded and the screen went dark, she could still see those amber eyes burning with some intense emotion that could have been joy or hope or fear. The whole experience had been disquieting but also fascinating, absorbing, puzzling. The smell of burning lasagna brought her back to the real world. *"Dio mio,"* she said to the big snake. "If I would just keep a dog or a monkey instead of you useless creatures, maybe I could get a little help with the housekeeping."

# thirteen

Fen was trying to communicate with the male Jackson's chameleon in its own language. The tiny lizard, Daria knew, was very angry. It had gone from pale green to almost black in less than a minute. Now a dramatic diamond pattern was beginning to emerge, and it was puffing itself up to look larger than it was. It turned sideways to Fen and rolled one of its eyes completely around so it could watch him. Fen, for his part, was running through a repertoire of what he regarded as friendly colors—greens, blues, pinks. He was not nearly so adept as the chameleon at patterns and accents, but he had a fine range of overall hues.

"I can't seem to cheer it up," Fen said. "This shade of blue is supposed to be very reassuring, but it doesn't seem to do anything for this little beast." He laid a gentle blue finger on the hanging vine that the chameleon was defending so valiantly and was rewarded with a feeble poke from all three of the creature's minuscule horns.

"It probably has a problem with the fact that in every other way, you don't look anything like a chameleon," Daria said. She was up in her loft bed—more or less trapped there by this early-morning visit of Fen's, although she knew that if she sat up stark naked in bed and groped around for something to put on, he wouldn't even notice. Fen had taken to coming in at almost any time of the day or night, a situation that Daria felt she ought to be able to control but somehow couldn't. He was so good at opening the lock on her door that it might as well not have been there, and he paid no attention to the sign commanding would-be entrants to knock. Fen, of course, knew that there were no dangerous animals loose inside. There was very little that he didn't know after a week of observation and relentless questioning, but Daria still worried about his judgment and implored him not to visit her room in her absence. Fen promised, for what that was worth.

"He's a brave little thing, isn't he?" Fen said. The chameleon had charged his finger again, this time emitting a nearly inaudible but no less furious hiss.

"Terribly brave, if not too bright," Daria said, "but this amount of stress isn't really good for chameleons, Fen. See if you can find the spray bottle and give his leaves a little shower so he can have a drink and calm down."

Fen's search for the spray bottle in the confusion on and under the big table gave Daria a chance to find a tunic in the crack between her bed and the wall. She yanked it over her head, climbed down the ladder, and began a quick tour of inspection while Fen sprayed the chameleon and the foliage in which it perched. Chameleons would only drink from drips and had been known to die of thirst in the presence of bowls of water if the rest of their environment was dry. They were contrary little things, fascinating and hard to raise. "Do you have chameleons on Chela?" Daria asked. She should have known better, but it was still very early in the morning.

"Of course not," Fen said.

"I mean, do you have something like chameleons?" Daria said. "Honestly, Fen, this is too exasperating. Don't you think we could just agree that I know Chelan animals are not exact copies of Terran animals and are classified differently and so on? Then when I say something like do you have bears or snakes or chickens or whatever, the whole conversation wouldn't have to come to a dead standstill for the millionth time while you explained it all over again. It would be refreshing, and it would speed things up, although there are times when I think the more obstacles you can throw in the way of my curiosity about Chelan animals the happier you are."

"Utter nonsense," Fen said. "I just want you to remember that there are no exact correspondences, any more than there are between you and me."

"You can say that again," Daria said crossly, "and so?"

"So what?"

"Chameleonlike animals on Chela, Fen."

"Not really. Lizardlike animals, yes, but color change

seems to have been reserved for the higher orders."

"How about civets?" Daria said. "Excuse me. How about civetlike animals?" She was watching the binturongs wind down for their long daytime sleep, trundling around their enclosure, the little male as close behind the female as he could get, both of them poking their long black noses under rocks and clumps of leaves in the hope of finding one last treat from the selection Daria had hidden the night before.

"Civets?" Fen said. "I don't think so."

Daria turned sharply and stared at him. "You don't think so? What do you mean, you don't think so?"

Fen's color darkened from a quite cheerful medium green to something much less agreeable—dead moss, perhaps, or beached seaweed. "I mean just that," he said. "I mean maybe there are but probably not. What am I supposed to be, a walking textbook of Chelan zoology? Civets are a pretty obscure family. How am I supposed to know if we have another obscure family that is somewhat like them?"

"I'm sorry," Daria said. "I didn't mean to get you all hot and bothered. I thought it was an easy question for someone as keen on zoology as you are."

"You're always nagging me to tell you about Chelan animals," Fen muttered.

"Am I? I thought I had been amazingly, stupendously, inhumanly quiet about it after the first few times you bit my head off, and I still don't see why I shouldn't ask and why you shouldn't answer."

"I don't either," Fen said with an obvious effort. "And I promise we will have a whole question-and-answer session soon. We'll sit down together, and you will ask anything you like, and I will answer to the best of my ability. How does that sound?"

"It sounds great. How about tonight after dinner?"

"I told Tim I would come and listen to his musical compositions."

"You won't be fit for much after that," Daria said, laughing. "Oh well. I'll hold you to it, Fen. Don't think I won't." She turned back to watch the binturongs climb into their bed, a process that always gave her special pleasure, perhaps because building their bed had been so much work.

The enclosure consisted mostly of sturdy climbing branches, since climbing is what binturongs do for entertainment, and at one point about five feet off the ground there was a place that practically begged to have a platform built on it. Still, it hadn't been easy to make a nest that was big and solid enough for some sixty pounds of animal, and Daria was proud of the result, which she had lined with dry palm fronds. The nest had met with immediate approval, and now the plump female clambered into it and curled up with her huge, bushy tail wound all the way around and up under her head for a pillow. The male followed and snuggled in the opposite direction so that they resembled two fuzzy, dark grey croissants with white-fringed ears. Soon the ears, too, were tucked in, and the binturongs were asleep for the day with their noses buried in each other's fur.

Fen had wandered over to look at the tamarins, and Daria heard him give a soft exclamation of surprise. His color had flared to an intense emerald, and he was standing on his toes staring up into the branches. "Look, Daria, look." Daria couldn't see a thing. She dragged the stool over beside Fen, which brought her head about level with his, and she could follow the long finger pointing into the leaves. After a moment she saw what he saw, namely Elfie looking smugly down at them and two lumps about the size of postage stamps on her back. The little monkey, after the fashion of her kind, had given birth to twins. While they watched, she plucked first one, then the other newborn from her back and plastered them to her breast.

"Clever Elfie, you've done it again," Daria said.

"Has she had babies before?"

"Tons of babies. Well, to be more precise, two every year for four years. That's tons by my standards." Daria slid off the stool and stood staring pensively in at the tamarins.

"You don't seem very happy about it," Fen said.

"Why wouldn't I be?" Daria said snappishly. "Of course I'm happy. It's just that the family is getting too big, and I promised Giovanna that as soon as another pair was born, she could have two pairs back. Now I have to decide which ones I can bear to part with. The answer is one, that I can't bear to part with any of them and two, that the choice is pretty obvious: Jake and Janice, Melvin and Milly, healthy young adults just about ready to breed."

"Not Milly," Fen cried. "Not Jake. Well, not Janice or Melvin either. We'll build another cage, Daria. I will help."

"That's sweet of you," Daria said, "and I know how you

feel, but it's missing the point. The problem isn't really space—not yet anyway. The problem is that the Ark has a fabulously successful program of returning mustached tamarins to the wild. It's working so well that soon they won't even need the captive breeding project. I don't want to think about that because then I'll be asked to breed something different in this terrific enclosure and have to give up all the mustaches. This, of course, is what it's all about, and I should be jumping up and down for joy and looking forward to having a new small primate."

"But it is natural to form attachments," Fen said, gazing sadly up into the branches where the four young tamarins were dashing around with three younger ones and Bernard, the father of the whole family.

"It's natural, and it isn't even discouraged. Keepers are supposed to love their animals and spend a lot of time thinking about how to make them happy and healthy and amused. But sometimes it seems like spending your life with a broken heart while your animals either die or get transferred."

"It can't be that bad," Fen said, appalled. "How many of your animals die, for example?"

"Plenty," Daria said. "Too many, even though I have a very good record. Of course, even one is too many when it comes to how you feel. Never mind, Fen. You're not destined to be a zookeeper, or I wouldn't think so."

"Probably not," Fen said, "but who knows? I can think of worse fates than settling down here and raising animals."

"Why here? Oh, that's right. You don't keep animals in

captivity on Chela. What would happen if you did? Would your head be chopped off?" Daria saw that Fen was halfway to the door, and she felt a little sorry for her remarks. He had been a good companion this morning. In fact, it was getting so he only drove her crazy about half the time now.

"Nothing quite so drastic as that," Fen said. "I'll see you later, Daria."

"Quite a lot later, as a matter of fact," Daria said. "I have to go shopping for school clothes with Mom and Lily. Ugh. I can't see what's wrong with the ones I've got. Your turn will be next, I should think. They'll have to take you to the big and tall shop, and that stuff will fit you like a tent. What a blast."

"I still don't see why I have to wear clothes at all," Fen complained.

"Well, you do, if you want to go to school."

"Suppose I don't want to go to school?"

Daria stared. "I thought you were an exchange student," she said. "That means you go to school with us, and we go to school with you. When is the second part going to happen, by the way, and who gets invited? I wouldn't have to nag you about Chelan animals if I could go and have a look for myself, though who would take care of the menagerie in my absence is hard to imagine."

"I wouldn't worry about it," Fen said. "I don't think it's going to happen very soon, especially if going to school is your idea of an exchange program. We don't have schools."

"What do you do? Learn from computers? We tried that for a while, but people got to missing teachers and getting together in groups and all the sentimental stuff that goes with school, so they started the whole thing up again, at least that's the way I understand it. For me it's a drag because I really don't have time. Well, you can imagine."

"Each Chelan child has a mentor who is always available," Fen explained, "so that when you don't understand something, you can ask, or you can have a philosophical discussion or tell some jokes or whatever seems good at the time of meeting, but the acquisition of knowledge is an individual matter. The concept of a classroom strikes us as tedious in the extreme."

"So if you didn't come here to go to school, what did you come for?" Daria asked.

Fen looked uneasy but answered briskly enough. "For cultural enrichment, obviously."

"It's not obvious to me, but I don't have time to sort it out." Daria crawled under the table and emerged with a pair of serviceable sandals. "Right now this lamb must be off to the slaughter. Please don't come in while I'm gone, Fen. I know you can, and I know you can't see why not, but it makes me really nervous, so please?"

"Rest assured," said Fen.

Daria returned in the early afternoon after a truly harrowing morning of shopping and went to seek the solace of her room. Fen was nowhere to be seen, which was a relief. She could have her animals to herself for once. The first thing was to check up on the baby foxes. Fen was dying to see them, and she was equally determined that the mother fox was not going to have the head of an alien poking into her den. "They'll be out soon," she had told him, "and unspeakably cute once their fur starts to come in. You'll be able to watch them all day long." And with that he had had to be satisfied.

She was getting good at the wriggle under the thorn bush and also no longer felt the need to be quiet. Snippet was quite calm now and seemed pleased to see her human friend. There were three kits, still with their eyes shut tight, nestled at her teats. "Move over, Snippet," Daria said. "Somebody's missing." She moved the foxes as gently as she could and shone the flashlight into the dark corners of the den. The space was small; there was really no place to lose even a very tiny kit, alive or dead. Daria lay on her stomach with her chin propped on her arms and stared in at the animals. It was hard to imagine what could have happened. She could only conclude that the dog fox had eaten one of the kits. Both Daria and Giovanna had felt that this father was unlikely to cannabalize his family. It was not common behavior for foxes, and Salim was happy and well-fed. Besides, why now and why only one?

Disturbed and mystified, Daria extracted herself from the fox pen and went off to the kitchen to start the evening food trolley. To her surprise Fen was there. He was putting a bottle of milk back in the refrigerator, which was odd since milk was almost the only Terran food he didn't like. This, plus the way he jumped when she came into the room, was enough to give pause to a person who had just lost a baby animal. He picked up a very small pitcher from the counter with exaggerated casualness and carried it toward the door. Daria moved into his path.

"Milk, Fen?" she said. "I thought milk was the last thing you would choose in this cornucopia of delights."

"A person can change his mind, I hope."

"Of course. I do it all the time. But if you have become a milk addict, that's an awfully small amount. Besides, you can get drink-size cartons from the slots, which are actually better tasting. That's milk Dad mixed from powder for something he was cooking. Here, let's pour the wimpy thing out and get you some proper milk."

Fen clutched the pitcher to his chest and glared at Daria. He had turned almost black, and while there was no real resemblance, he reminded her of a badger she had once seen being harried by a dog. "You are a most interfering person," he said. "You nag; you tease; you insinuate. And I wish you would leave me alone for a few minutes. If I want to drink this tiny amount of milk from the refrigerator, what possible difference can it make to you?"

Thoroughly taken aback, Daria said, "Golly, Fen. None, I guess," and stepped out of the doorway through which he charged, slopping milk at her feet as he passed. She was now reasonably sure what had become of the baby fox, an idea that infuriated, amused, and baffled her in nearly equal proportions. It was hard to know what to do, and a relief to have her father appear at the garden door.

"Dad, guess what?" she said. "I'm almost sure our guest from outer space has abducted one of my baby foxes."

Roger was carrying a basket of early strawberries from

the garden, which he put down carefully before turning to face his daughter. "Well, that's a poser, isn't it?" he said. "What makes you think so? I know. One is missing, and Fen is acting guilty."

"That's about it, if you add acting guilty while carrying off a tiny pitcher of milk from the refrigerator—cooking milk, by the way, and not something he even likes. What am I supposed to do? If I ask him, he'll lie. Oh, and he's gone very hostile all of a sudden, which is also suggestive and makes any kind of discussion impossible."

"Well, let's have a look in his room," Roger said. "You should be able to set aside your privacy scruples on this occasion."

"Without a qualm," Daria said. "Let's go."

They accessed Fen's room from the main console in the living room, which afforded them a fine one-way view. He was sitting on the edge of his bed with a pillow in his lap. His skin was a soft, almost luminous green. One long-fingered hand held an eyedropper of milk, the other an infant fox, its eyes shut tight, squealing and stretching out for the next drop.

"Holy hippos," Daria said. "That's not even the right kind of milk. He'll probably kill it. Call me a coward, Dad, but please come with me to the rescue."

Roger put a restraining hand on his daughter's arm. "Let's think this through," he said.

"What's to think about? That baby needs to be back on its mother's teat but fast."

"Would she accept it back?"

"God, I hope so. Yes, probably. Fennecs aren't that fussy."

"Now think about Fen," Roger said. "Have you ever seen that shade of green before? I would say he is in a state as near to total bliss as we can imagine short of religious ecstasy. No wonder he was rude to you. He must be in a panic that you will take his pet away and also that he may not be doing the right things to keep it alive. Fennecs can be hand-reared, can't they?"

"Yes, but . . ."

"Then let him do it, Daria. Take him some proper milk and give him a few lessons in baby animal nurture. He'll be a quick study."

"Foxes make terrible pets," Daria said, switching defenses. "They're unbelievably destructive. By the time this little darling is six weeks old, assuming it survives, the guest room will be in shreds."

Roger grinned. "As if you cared."

"Well, that's true. I don't, but still, you have no idea how much trouble they can be. I doubt Fen has the patience."

"Do you?"

"No, actually, I don't," Daria said crossly. "He's probably got the patience of a saint." She was staring again through the monitor at Fen. He put the eyedropper carefully on the bedside table and gently stroked the tiny animal's rear end. The kit obligingly urinated on the pillow. Smiling beatifically, Fen slowly stretched out on his bed, and the baby fox, mewing and warbling piteously, made its way up his chest and down into the hollow of his neck, where it promptly fell asleep.

"I'll have to ask Giovanna," Daria said. "After all, I'm breeding fennec foxes, not just playing with them, but she'll probably take your side. She will think it interesting and worth the risk. Why do all the adults in my life make me feel as if I'm about ninety?"

"Well, first they dump a whole lot of responsibility on your shoulders, and then they stand back and chuckle while you worry."

Daria snapped off the computer. "That must be it. Well, let them have their beauty sleep. I'm going to get some puppy formula and then figure out a diplomatic way to give it to Fen."

"He will be relieved," Roger said. "After his initial outrage, of course. Have fun. Help yourself to strawberries in the kitchen, but don't take too many for the animals. Those are the first of the season."

Roger was off to his studio, up the spiral staircase at the front of the house. Daria watched him go with a mixture of exasperation and affection. Did he ever fail to get his way? No. Was he always right? Surely not. And with the alien they were all on such shaky ground. "I wish..." Daria said to the empty room, but then couldn't think what it was she wished. She went back to the kitchen and began to assemble the animals' evening meal, a simple task and, in its way, a soothing one. When she had put the last portion on the trolley, Daria brought down a box marked "puppy milk" from a high shelf and put it on top of the load.

# fourteen

Fen was beginning to wish that he had not elected to lie down. He was much too excited to sleep and was also afraid to move for fear of waking the infinitely precious, tiny creature that slumbered with her nose in his ear. Her breath tickled, and he was getting a stiff neck, but he was gloriously happy. He knew the situation was fraught with problems—that Daria would certainly have a fit and probably try to take his baby away, that he might not have the right feeding formula for an infant fox, that there were at least a hundred important things he didn't know. Figuring this was one problem he could solve without moving too much, he groped for the remote control to access the Net.

With the perversity that Fen believed characterized the female of his species, Filya picked this moment to call. He heard the communicator buzz and cursed the fact that he had, as usual, hidden it under his pillow. Tempted to ignore the summons but knowing that by doing so he would break the first article of the oath the nine young Chelans had sworn, he groped and found the device without waking the kit.

Filya was lonely, and apparently it was Fen's fault. "Why don't you ever call me?" she asked. "I've waited four days. Don't you know it is humiliating for the female to always be the one who calls?"

"I don't see why," Fen said, genuinely puzzled. "I should think it has more to do with who is busiest, and as it happens, I have been very busy indeed."

"So have I," Filya said with a small, forced laugh. "Paola has finally managed to take me shopping. What do you think?"

Fen squinted at the little screen, which still showed only Filya's head, and wondered what he was supposed to say. Then slowly she pulled back so that he could see all of her. "You're wearing clothes."

"I had to, Fen. They wouldn't let me out of the house. In fact, the first thing was that a tailor came here and made me something I could wear to the store. Isn't that ridiculous? But, really, what do you think?" Filya raised her arms and turned slowly through the beginning passages of one of Chela's most seductive ritual courtship dances, and the long tunic swirled about her body. Fen enlarged his monitor and stared at his friend. He still couldn't see that the tunic was any improvement but was wise enough not to say so.

"Interesting," he said. "Different. You may grow to like it."

"I confess I already do. Why are you lying there like that, stiff as a stick?"

Fen smiled, not, he hoped, too smugly. "Look closely near my right ear."

Filya peered and gasped. "What is it? It looks like a baby mammal of some sort. Oh, Fen, what have you done?"

"Made off with a week-old fennec fox kit."

"Does Daria know?"

"If she doesn't now, she will any minute," Fen said gloomily. "She looks in at those babies about ten times a day, and when she misses one, the shit is going to hit the windmill, as they say here for some reason."

"How will she know you took it?"

"She won't immediately, but the possibilities are limited and privacy nonexistent. They carry on about the sanctity of their living quarters, but the minute they really want to peek, it's flip a switch, twirl a dial, and there they are, practically in bed with you."

"Don't be cross," Filya said. "This should be the happiest moment of your life. Oh dearest Fen, please let me see a little better. It's so tiny, and the light is so bad. Would it be a terrible thing to pick it up?"

"She needs to sleep," Fen said, and then after a look at Filya's stricken face, "but maybe she won't wake up if I am careful." He cupped his hand around the kit and sat up slowly on the edge of the bed. At last she was curled in the palm of his hand, still sleeping under the strong overhead light. "Her eyes are still closed, and she hasn't any hair," Fen whispered. "She drinks milk just a drop at a time from an eyedropper. Her name is Scrabble. Please don't ask me why. And oh, Filya, I wish you were here to share this with me."

Filya sighed, and a single tear rolled down the soft green curve of her cheek. "This baby will be almost grown by the time we meet to go home," she said. "But by then you will have many other animals, including, I should think, some more very little ones for me and the others to pet and care for."

Fen should have been prepared for this, but he was not. Taking Earth animals back to Chela, he knew already, was not going to work. They were not going to be able to buy, borrow, or steal a pair of this and a pair of that and stuff them into their spaceship. He could almost see Daria's face, incredulous at the very idea, and he could see that Filya, at least, had her heart set on it. Had she told the others of his situation? And what about the others? For all he knew, one of them might have landed in a place where there were even more animals.

"Please, Filya, don't jump to conclusions," he said, "and try to forgive me. I have been derelict in my duties to the Group. It has all been much too exciting for me, and I have not thought through the consequences."

"That is perfectly understandable," Filya said magnanimously. "I, too, would have been incapacitated by excitement. Now, however, the time has arrived for constructive thought and concerted action. A conference call is in order. When will you be ready?"

"Sometime next month?"

"Very funny."

"Day after tomorrow," Fen conceded. "Late in the day so I have time to organize my thoughts. Tomorrow I am going with Daria to the Hudson Valley Ark, a very large facility for the breeding of endangered animals. I will include that experience in my report. I will show my little fox, and I will try to be where there are other animals for everyone to see."

"Which is more than you've done for me," Filya said.

"By the Guardians, you are a pushy wench. How long have we been here? Not much more than a week, of which every day has been so full I have hardly had time to eat, much less sleep the required amount."

"Well, don't let me take up any more of your time," Filya said. "After all, who am I? Merely your betrothed future mate. Take no notice of my needs. I should be quite content here with this lovely family that spends half its time thinking about food and the other half worrying about clothes."

Fen jumped to his feet the better to roar at his beloved and woke the fox kit, who began to wail and snuffle blindly for the comfort of her mother's belly or, failing that, for the hollow of Fen's neck. She also appeared to be hungry again.

"Now look what you've done," Filya said. "But how nice for me to see her awake. Fen, do something for the poor baby. It's breaking my heart." Fen laid the kit down between two pillows on his bed, a cozy enough spot that only caused her to squall more piteously.

Both Chelans were now seriously alarmed, nor were they soothed by the sound of a sharp rap on Fen's door. "Guardians and demons protect me," Fen muttered. "That has to be Daria. Farewell, dear Filya. I'll let you know what happens, if I survive." He snapped the communicator off, shoved it under the pillow by the shrieking kit, and opened the door. The hall was empty but for a small packet of powdered milk, a bottle of sterile water, a bowl, a spoon, and a note. "This is puppy milk and correct for foxes," the note read. "Rubbing its bottom after meals is right (though I wonder how you knew) and what its mother would do with her tongue if she had a chance. It needs to be cuddled a lot. The horrendous noises are normal. We must talk when I am less furious. Daria."

The urgent needs of baby animals leave one little time to brood. Fen spent less than a minute on his conflicting feelings of gratitude, annoyance, and embarrassment. Daria had obviously been spying on his efforts to care for Scrabble. The fact that she had decided to allow him to do it was inexplicable and miraculous. Meanwhile, he'd better mix up some puppy milk and get it into his pet without delay, hoping that exhaustion and a full stomach would persuade her to sleep in her nest of pillows until he could devise some sort of pouch to carry her in.

Fen set to work. He mixed the powdered milk and spent a blissful half hour giving it to Scrabble one drop at a time. He massaged Scrabble's bottom until she peed, and at last she fell asleep between the pillows. The problem of a pouch yielded with surprising ease once he started to roam around the house with an open mind. The fact that Terran females carried leather pouches of various sizes and left them lying on tables and chairs was a boon. The fact that the perfect pouch happened to be Lily's was a misfortune Fen would only come to appreciate later. He turned the sparse contents of the bag out gently on the coffee table and went outside to find some soft grass to line it with.

"Good afternoon, Peru. *Buenas dias, Colombia!*" Daria, in a moment of uncharacteristic levity, had told him that the female llama, having recently arrived from South America, understood only Spanish, so Fen, for whom languages were not a major problem, had added Spanish to his rapidly growing list of things to learn. Colombia, perhaps due to the language barrier, was inclined to be standoffish, but big-hearted Peru was always good for a nuzzle and a hug.

"Let me have some of this soft undercoat, Peru," Fen said. "Some that's already loose, of course." Peru nibbled his shoulder while, by dint of vigorous petting, Fen acquired a handful of wonderful, soft llama wool.

Scrabble would have a luxury nest. He sat down on a rock and began to line the pouch, humming a popular Chelan tune as he worked. It was a song particularly dear to Filya, since it described the nesting activities of a pair of betrothed Chelans. To most Terrans it would have suggested a chorus of several thousand hungry female mosquitoes. To Tim, however, as he wandered past on his way to the carport, the song was interesting, if far from beautiful, even by his standards.

"What kind of a song is that?" Tim asked, and Fen, who

had been unaware of his presence, jumped a foot.

"Song? What song? Oh, you mean my little hum. It's part of a long and rather boring courtship cycle. Do you like it?"

"I feel it might grow on me."

"Well, I'll sing you some more sometime, but I warn you it's pretty repetitive, and I am not a very good singer. Perhaps you will get to hear Binya before we all go back. She is another exchange student and a wonderful singer who commands a hundred times the overtones of someone like me."

Tim felt the hairs rise on the back of his neck. "That sounds awesome," he said, "but maybe it would be better to get into it in a small way by listening to you. I say, is that Lily's pocketbook you're stuffing with old hair?"

"It might be," Fen admitted. "I have this almost newborn baby fox, and she needs a nest that I can carry around since she is unwilling to be separated from me. I just picked up the first pouch I saw that looked to be the right size and shape."

"Man, you have a death wish," Tim said. "I'd paint it blue with polka dots or something and hope she doesn't recognize it. What did you do with the contents?"

"There wasn't much. What there was I placed with great care on the coffee table."

"I wish you all the best," said Lily's twin, turning toward the carport, "and maybe you've been lucky. If there wasn't much in the bag, she must be using another one. But take my advice, old man, paint it blue."

Fen smiled and gave the soft wool a final pat. He was not afraid of Lily or of any human being, with the possible exception of Daria. This thought gave him pause. Daria was a small and really quite unaggressive female person. Why should he be so alarmed at the prospect of her displeasure? Probably because Daria had so much to give and so much to withhold, and even though he had learned (in about two seconds' time) to enter her room when it was locked, he still needed her and tried to cultivate her friendship. Usually. "I probably set myself back six months with Daria," Fen muttered. "What a dumb thing to do." But the fact was that once he had made his illicit visit to the mother fox and her family, there had been no help for it. A fennec kit had become—instantly and without appeal to reason—essential to his existence.

"And that being the case," he commented to Peru, who had wandered back to see if he needed anything, "I'd better get back to my room without delay."

# fifteen

Fen gazed at Giovanna Ferrante across a table laden with simple goodies—the best the Ark had to offer a hungry young traveler from space. Haute cuisine was not one of the amenities of a cafeteria designed to feed hard-working zoologists, keepers, and gardeners, which was why Giovanna often dined at home. What it lacked in finesse, however, the cafeteria made up for in location. Its long-windowed dining room and terrace were in the center of an elegant low building of native stone that curved along the brow of a cliff overlooking the Hudson. Dwarf pines and flowering shrubs softened the severe grey walls. Giovanna had been giving Fen a tour while Daria settled the four tamarins in with the others that were being taught to forage for themselves and otherwise readied for their trip to the Amazon. Her trained eye had detected Fen's flagging metabolism before he had been aware of it himself, and she had brought him here to sit in the warm spring sunshine, to refuel and perhaps to divulge a fraction of the information she lusted after.

At the moment he was recovering from the sight of some eighty species of animals singly and in pairs, families, troops, and battalions, ranging from frogs the size of a fingernail to four-ton rhinos. He was also consuming his first peanut butter sandwich, an oversight of the Wells family that was difficult to explain or condone. Scrabble slumbered in Lily's purse on his lap, having been fed earlier by an obliging canid keeper.

"Delicious," Fen said. "Delectable. And I am quite revived. Is there more that I should see?"

"With animals there is always more," Giovanna said. "We could retrace our steps exactly, and you would see a hundred things that had changed in the past hour. But in terms of facilities, no. Only this building. This building is in many ways the most remarkable place in the Ark, and I will be delighted to show it to you, but first I think you owe me some satisfaction of my own curiosity."

The young alien shifted in his chair, and his color darkened, then lightened again, as if he made a conscious effort to be calm. His long fingers strayed to the amulet on his chest. "You wanted to see this thing," he muttered. "It is hard to imagine why, but of course you may, if it interests you."

He still made no move to take it off, and Giovanna waited with a naturalist's patience until at last he met her eyes, gave a very human shrug of his bony shoulders, and slipped the chain over his head.

No lab work was needed for Giovanna to see that the object was a tooth and the chain was gold. Chelan gold, she suspected, was much like Terran gold, and this had that eighteen-carat look—a heavy and valuable setting for a slightly ratty-looking animal tooth. Keeping her face impassive, she handed the amulet back to Fen, who slipped it on with an indifferent gesture that wouldn't have deceived a child. "Thank you," Giovanna said. "I apologize for being so inquisitive over so personal a matter. We zoologists are perhaps abnormally attracted by such artifacts of the animal kingdom—teeth, bones, bits of hair. We can't help wondering, you know, about the original owners."

The amber eyes stared almost hypnotically into hers. "I wish I could help you," Fen said, "but since I believed, and indeed still believe, that the thing is plastic, the question of animal origin would not have occurred to me."

"Of course it wouldn't," Giovanna said heartily, "and thank you for putting up with the curiosity of an old snoop. Now on to the really interesting stuff."

"Which is?"

"The animals of Chela, of course. You promised to tell me all about them, and while I understand that this would probably take weeks, months, or years, we can make a start. Jonathan!" she called to a young keeper who was about to sit down at a nearby table, "Be a darling and bring our guest a chocolate milkshake."

"I am no longer hungry," Fen said, and indeed his color

was far from good. It was interesting, Giovanna thought, how quickly one adapted to the biology of another race. If anyone had asked her a week ago what colors were healthy or unhealthy for a Chelan, she would have been at a loss to answer.

"Cancel the milk shake," she called to Jonathan. "Why is this such a difficult topic for you? *Avanti,* my friend! I know you are not a zoologist. Just describe a few animals for me. Maybe you have a pet or some other favorite animal that you know well. Am I asking so much?"

Fen, who had been staring down at the table during this barrage, seemed to rally and draw strength from some inner source. The dark, muddy ocher ebbed from his skin, leaving it a uniform, silvery grey. "Of course not," he said. "The problem is one that I experienced with Daria, whom I offended deeply. Naturally, I would prefer not to offend you in the same way."

"People of my age are much harder to offend than sixteen-year-olds."

"It's just that we don't believe in keeping animals in any kind of captivity," he said. "So we have no pets or domestic animals, and we don't have wonderful institutions like this. The result is somewhat like, well, two nations coexisting on the same planet. The animals live in the wild, and we live in towns. We don't see much of each other," he finished rather lamely.

Whatever Giovanna had expected to hear, this improbable tale of two nations was not it. She stared at her visitor open-mouthed. "You have no contact with the animals of your world? I am surprised that some don't simply come to live with you as the dog and the cat did long ago on Earth—as, in a less symbiotic sense, the squirrel, the raccoon, the deer, the pigeon, to name only a few, have moved in with us. What have you done—put domes around your cities to keep the animals out?" She saw that she had upset him again and was glad. She wanted answers now, and she was beginning to remember replays of this conversation that had taken place between other Chelans and the first explorers of their world.

"We have done nothing to keep the animals out," Fen said angrily. "They simply live their own lives, and we live ours."

"And is this why," Giovanna asked gently, "one of the first things you did upon coming to Earth was to purloin an infant animal, despite the enormous work and inconvenience this act entailed and the fact that it was almost certain to anger a very important person in your life?"

"I am atypical," Fen said. "I confess to being interested in animals and to wishing that I had closer contact with them."

"Evidently." Giovanna smiled and leaned back in her chair. Again the silence lengthened between them. Fen sat with his arms folded across his chest—cool, grey, impenetrable—for about a minute and a half. Then, as if biologically throwing caution to the wind, he turned a fierce magenta from head to foot.

"Being atypical," he said, "I have, of course, a favorite

animal. If I describe it to you, will you let me off for a while and show me some more of the Ark?"

"Yes."

Fen took a deep breath and began to speak. "It is called the mir-akona, and it is very beautiful. Like many Chelan animals, its coat is blue, but the mir-akona is the only one of this particular shade—a medium to dark blue tinged with lavender. The insides of its ears are almost black with a white fringe, and its tail is like this, too—a very dark blue with a white tassel on the end. It is a little larger, and especially longer, than one of your domestic cats and graceful like a cat but even more so. I love to watch it hunt small rodents through the grass. It is also beautiful when it sleeps on a tree branch with its long black nose hanging down one side and its silver-tipped tail down the other."

Giovanna sighed. "You make me long to see one, though perhaps I am too old for interplanetary travel. I will have to look into it. But tell me more about this lovely beast. It sounds much like a Terran mammal. Are its young born live?"

"Of course."

"Not of course at all. It might be a monotreme like the platypus and lay eggs—like you yourself when it comes to that."

"True," Fen said, and turned, if possible, an even more intense shade of magenta.

"What is its gestation period? How many young does it have? Are they helpless at birth or somewhat independent?"

"Please, Dr. Ferrante, I am not able to answer detailed zoological questions. I have admired the mir-akona with binoculars from the edge of the forest. I know what it looks like and how it moves. I know that it is very beautiful and that I, and that I . . . You will have to excuse me," Fen said in a strangled voice, and buried his face in his hands.

His color was fading to grey again. After a long moment Giovanna reached out and stroked one of the fragile, attenuated wrists. "I am truly sorry," she said. "The whole subject of animals is obviously fraught with emotions that I am unable to understand and should respect."

"Not really," Fen mumbled, but Giovanna knew he lied. She had stumbled upon a very great mystery, but it would be cruel and probably useless to pursue it further at this time.

"In any event," she went on, "you were brought here to be entertained and instructed, not tormented. Can you guess what this building is for?"

Fen raised his head. "Administration? Computers? Laboratories?"

"All that and much, much more. The future of many endangered species is in this building, Fen, as well, perhaps, as that of some already gone from Earth."

Fen drew a sharp breath. "Sperm and ova banks," he said.

"And DNA of other sorts."

"You can re-create an extinct animal?"

"If we have enough organic material, yes we can and we have. It is easier with the more recently extinct; there's more to work with."

Giovanna, who had looked lions in the eye at this distance without flinching, almost cringed in the light that blazed from the yellow eyes of her young visitor. "So if an animal becomes extinct," he said, "it's no big deal. You just make some more?"

Giovanna didn't know whether to laugh or cry. She thought of her beloved squirrel monkey and of a hundred others she had known intimately that were now gone. "What a splendid fantasy!" she said. "Forgive me. I can see that you reached a logical conclusion from what I said, but you are wrong. We can re-create an animal, even a pair of animals, but a whole species, no. You vastly overestimate our resources and technology. What you suggest is still entirely in the realm of the theoretical."

"I must see these facilities at once," Fen said, as if he hadn't heard her last remarks. "I find this research intensely interesting."

So for the next hour Giovanna led her guest through the laboratories and storage banks of the Hudson Valley Ark. It was hard to tell, but he seemed to sort, categorize, and file away for easy reference every single item of information that came his way. In a spirit of experimentation, Giovanna gradually increased the difficulty of her discourse. It made no difference. He continued to look and listen with the same intent but unstrained concentration.

She skipped lightly over the administrative offices, knowing that they would interest him least, but insisted on explaining at length the vast computer programs that now kept track of every captive animal in the world. "Look,

Fen," she said, stepping up to one of the monitors and beginning to poke the keys. "This is an obvious example, but not long ago I needed to know what was going on in the world of baby white rhinos. Here we are in Johannesburg a month before our baby was born. They had a tough time, but it turned out all right in the end." The screen showed a premature infant rhinoceros in an incubator surrounded by people in white coats. Then it showed the same baby nursing from its gigantic mother. "Everyone was watching," Giovanna went on, "zoo people from all over the world, and everyone was sure that it would die or that if it survived, it would have to be hand-reared. Lots of drama, lots of fun, as well as some new veterinary techniques for those of us who weren't doing the work and the worrying. Even more important is stuff like this." The picture of the little rhino and its mother was replaced with pages of genealogical charts, graphs, and lists. "All to be consulted before we bring a pair of animals together to mate, all to be added to after the blessed event," Giovanna said.

Fen appeared to find all this fascinating. Indeed there was nothing about the long building on the cliff that did not interest him, including the security arrangements, which, his guide told him, had to be strict. "Most people think we are doing useful work and should be left alone to do it," Giovanna explained, "but there are still plenty of loonies, some of them potentially very destructive. Genetic research is the prime target, so the gene banks and laboratories need to be particularly well locked up."

Fen himself, Giovanna thought, might, but for his intelligence and the formidable screening that must have gone into his selection as a visitor to Earth, be among the dangerous fanatics. He couldn't seem to see enough of the sperm and ova banks and the endless little freezer drawers of tissue saved for its DNA. As a spectacle, Giovanna thought it rather dull, and while only the actual containers were kept below freezing, the rooms were cold. The young Chelan appeared not to notice. His virtually naked body a shimmering, silvery green, he stood and stared with burning eyes at the long corridors of drawers, floor to ceiling, rank upon rank, down nearly the entire length of the North Wing. The drawers were numbered and gave no indication of their contents.

"As you might expect, we need a good, fast, foolproof program for finding things." Giovanna went to another terminal and looked inquiringly at Fen. "Give me a request, just off the top of your head."

Fen came up beside her, standing very close where he could see every detail on the monitor. In the cold room his body seemed to give off heat as if he had a fever, but his voice was calm, almost casual. "How about Scrabble's father," he said.

Giovanna spoke to the computer. "*Canidae,*" she said. "*Vulpes zerda,* two thousand ninety-three." Long lists scrolled down the screen and stopped at a short group of names. Fen saw "Daria Wells" in a column under the heading "Private Breeders," and "Salim" under "Breeding Males." This was followed by a date in the year 2093 and a number. "So, we took sperm from Salim on February 10, 2093,"

Giovanna continued. "Now here's a neat feature—a frill, really, but nice for visitors or people in a hurry. Location, please. Look down the hall, Fen."

He did as he was told and saw a bright blue light at the end of one of the rows of drawers and a blinking red arrow pointing down the row to the left. Following the arrow, he came to an illuminated drawer bearing the same number he had seen on the computer screen.

"There you are," Giovanna said. "Or rather, there is Salim in all his glory, in case we ever need him. Yes, what is it, Edwina?"

A young chimpanzee had come through the door in the back of the sperm bank. She approached Giovanna, jumped up and down once, and handed her a note.

"Thank you, Edwina, my dear." The director fished in voluminous pockets, produced a carrot, and handed it to the messenger, who then bounded away. "Your family is getting restless, Fen."

"Let them wait," Fen said.

Giovanna laughed. "Oh, Fen, let them not wait. You have seen enough for one day. Besides, this old woman is frozen nearly stiff. Let's go back out in the sun. I don't know how you stand it with hardly a stitch on."

Fen glanced down at his body, which was covered with very human-looking goose bumps, and suddenly began to shiver uncontrollably. He followed Giovanna out onto the sunny terrace with only one wistful backward glance.

Daria and Tim were already there, at a table near the wall and the stupendous view out over the river to Bear

Mountain. Daria, looking gloomy and with smudges on her cheeks that had not been there when they had arrived, was pawing listlessly through a salad. Tim sat across from her, smiling benignly at a tall stein of beer.

"Join us," Tim said. "Have some nourishment."

Fen and Giovanna ducked into the cafeteria and emerged with two trays, on one a cup of espresso and a tiny glass of grappa, on the other a hamburger, French fries, a beer, and chocolate cake.

"That should fortify you," Tim said. "What's the matter? You look cold."

"Fen is more interested in the gene banks than I could possibly have imagined," Giovanna said. "We went unprepared for a polar expedition."

Daria located a pallid chunk of tomato in her salad and ate it, meanwhile gazing with undisguised hostility at Fen's rare burger. "For anyone who likes animals so much, you certainly don't have much of a problem with eating them," she said.

Fen gave her a stern look. "Like you, I am an omnivore," he said. "Omnivores require animal protein."

"They don't require it to be bleeding all over their plates."

"To me it seems that disguising meat or cooking it until it has no taste is ridiculously hypocritical."

"I don't disguise meat. I just don't eat it. Neither would you if you used an ounce of imagination about where it comes from."

"I find it hard to be critical of Fen's enthusiasm for our meat," Giovanna said. "If the reports from his planet are correct, the Chelans have no meat at all—only elaborate simulations of meat created from high-protein vegetable matter. No one knows why this should be true, and the Chelans themselves are extremely reticent on the subject."

"Nothing like spoiling a guy's lunch, you two," Tim commented, and indeed Fen did appear to have lost his appetite. He dropped his fork, which clattered onto the stone pavement, and stumbled to his feet. The rosy hue with which he had begun his meal had darkened to an angry, blackened red. In a moment he pushed his chair over with a crash and rushed away.

The three humans watched him go, his long strides taking him in seconds around the end of the North Wing and out of sight. "What did we do?" Daria cried. "I'm sorry, but I don't see why a little argument about meat eating should set him off like that."

"It would be interesting to speculate," Giovanna said, "but let's find him first. I'll alert the staff." She spoke quietly into the small communicator that hung around her neck, studied its display for a moment as the map lit up with the locations of nearly a hundred Ark personnel on duty that day, and snapped it shut. "I'm assuming he's not dangerous," she went on. "God knows he looks frightening enough, but I don't want anyone to overreact. He's not a polar bear after all."

"I don't think he would hurt a fly," Daria said. "Which is not to say he hasn't scared me out of my wits a few times. I've seen him almost this upset before, though never quite such an awful color."

"What does he do to make himself feel better?"

"At our place he usually goes out to the pond," Daria said. "He'll go over to the side away from the house and sit on the bank watching the water birds or talking to Peru, who always seems to know when a spot of comfort is needed. It never takes long before he's his old pink, cheerful, nosy self again."

"Well, if he's talking to the ducks or the llamas, he won't be lost for long," Giovanna said. "Still, I think I'll have a look around myself. I'm sorry I goaded him about Chelan dietary practices. Stupid of me."

Giovanna got up, and Daria joined her, saying, "I know what you mean. I did it, too. Let's tramp around. Tim can hold the fort and be a rallying point."

"Sounds good to me," Tim said. "My conscience is clear, at least when it comes to ill-chosen remarks about food."

Angry humans often say that they see red. For Fen it was the same—literally and with a vengeance. At the moment, as he charged around the corner of the laboratory building, it was as if the benign world of the Hudson Valley Ark had been bathed in blood. This was a dangerous state for Fen to be in, since both his vision and his judgment were impaired.

It was, therefore, a minor miracle that he managed to run several miles without plunging into a moat or decapitating himself on a branch. He fetched up in the lower reaches of the wolf woods, where a stream had been partially dammed to make a habitat for the short-clawed otters.

There was a strong plastic mesh fence to keep them in and a locked gate that held Fen up for about thirty seconds. Already the red veil before his eyes was beginning to clear, and he sank gratefully onto the bank to allow the sound of the stream and the quiet presence of old trees to restore his calm. There were no animals in sight, nor had there been a sign on the gate, since the Ark was designed not for visitors but for people who already knew what they had and where it was housed. For Fen, who was not afraid of animals even when he should have been, the absence of creatures inside the enclosure aroused neither disappointment nor curiosity. He had been drawn by the sound of running water. If animals emerged, so much the better.

Peace of mind, however, was not so easily won as he had come to expect from similar visits to the duck pond. Too emotional, he thought, too easily upset. The elders who had wanted to disqualify him had been right. He was no longer angry and wondered briefly what it had all been about. Oh yes, Daria's stupid talk about meat eating. This in itself would have been cause only for the sort of wrangle he rather enjoyed, but then Giovanna Ferrante, a person whom he all but worshiped, had made such unpleasant and insinuating remarks about the Chelan diet. He had squirmed under the gaze of those intelligent black eyes, and then he had flown into a rage. "Cretin!" Fen shouted to the woods. "Idiot. Fool." It seemed to him that, having by a miracle landed in the orbit of one of the greatest zoologists on Earth and gained her friendship and trust, he had thrown it all away in an instant of childish temper, and with it all access to the great banks of animal genetic material he had seen today.

Fen shut his eyes and let his head sink on his chest while one hand enclosed the tooth on its golden chain. At his side the tiny fox slumbered in her nest of llama wool. Softly, almost inaudibly, the young Chelan began the mantra of his cadre: "Ah kisiner, farlin, mir-akona, titikin, es-alana, tatacal, coplana . . ." The long roll call of Chelan animals went on, their musical names falling softly on the spring air of another planet.

There was a brief silence, as if a prayer had been offered under the cathedral of the trees. This was followed by a series of splashes, squeaks, and grunts as the Malaysian otters ended their afternoon nap. Sleek brown bodies flashed through dappled sunlight. They seemed to emerge from every crack and crevice on the bank across from Fen. They poured out of hollow logs and streamed between trees and rocks, hitting the water in piles of twisting, shining brown fur.

It would have been hard to find a better remedy for melancholy and self-reproach. Fen gave a shout of delight and waded into the water, not forgetting first to hang Scrabble around his neck instead of his waist. The otters withdrew and regrouped in a cave of tangled tree roots, but then they were off again, disregarding the alien presence in their pool and even sporting around the tall form in their midst.

It was thus that Giovanna and Daria found their lost exchange student. They came over the ridge to the south of the pond and stopped dead in their tracks. "*Jesu Maria,* those little bastards bite," Giovanna said.

"But not our alien friend. Nothing seems to bite Fen. I suppose his smell is totally unthreatening, but still it's weird." Daria scratched her head and stared down at Fen and the otters. "I hate to be a spoil sport, but I have to get home, and even Tim's patience must be wearing thin, or else he's getting too drunk to drive even on autopilot."

Still the two zoologists, one with more than fifty years of experience, the other just beginning her career, watched and could not bring themselves to call out to the shimmering green figure surrounded by romping aquatic mammals. In the end the decision was made by the smallest animal around. They saw Fen bend his head and peer into the pouch that hung against his chest. Then in a moment he was out of the water, through the gate, and up the hill. If he was surprised to see Daria and Giovanna, he gave no sign. "Scrabble is hungry," he said, and was off into the woods ahead of them, on course for the canid complex and the nearest source of puppy milk.

# sixteen

In the late afternoon of the next day, Fen gathered his communicator, his baby fox, and his notes, which were to prove useless in the excitement of the conference call, and repaired to the far side of the duck pond. There, perched on the bank at the edge of the woods, he went to work on his monitor screen, pulling and stretching until it reached the size he had been warned was the maximum attainable without pulling a hole in the fabric. He propped the silvery square against a tree, angling it toward the pond in the hope that his friends would be able to see the water birds. Perhaps Peru and Suzy would come if he called to them, and he would be able to share his own first experiences with the animals of Earth.

"Breathe deeply," Fen told himself. "Remain grey." He was surprised to find himself nervous, even a little frightened, at the prospect of seeing the members of the Group who were, apart from his family, closer to him than any other beings in the universe. It was a closeness that went beyond personality, beyond liking and disliking. They had been together since childhood, training for one event, thinking, talking, dreaming of nothing else. It was natural that he had picked his future mate from among the members of the Group. Others had done the same. Even on Chela they had been like a race apart, and now they were scattered across the face of an alien world. Fen's long fingers found the amulet on his chest and stroked the eroded surface of the tooth. His heart slowed, and his color stabilized. He focused on the screen. There was a sharp beep and a flash of light followed by nothing. Then Filya's voice but no image. Then, suddenly, they were all there at the same time, calling each other's names and laughing at the strangeness and delight of doing this thing that they had practiced between different rooms of the institute on Chela, but that no one had ever really believed could work across the seas and mountain ranges of another planet.

The overall effect was somewhat disquieting, since he could see slices of eight different environments to go with the eight Chelans. Despite attempts to keep the figures sharp and the backgrounds out of focus, it was hard not to stare at, for example, the elaborate tile roof of the Chinese temple before which Tendron smiled and waved. Filya had urged each of them to call from the most boring and nondescript setting that could be found—a blank wall or a treeless plain. Not one of the Group had followed her advice. Additionally, all but one of them held some kind of pet, the exception being Binya, who was mounted on a tall black horse. Filya herself held her little ginger cat and stood on the balcony with a spectacular view of Rome behind her. Fen thought she looked both imperious and confused. This was not leadership as she had so ably practiced it on Chela.

"You must try not to talk all at once," Filya said, her high, clear voice cutting through the babble of her friends. In the brief silence that followed this unpopular instruction, she went on. "I know all of you want to tell about your Terran families and the peculiar cultures you are living in and especially about your pets and the other animals you have seen, but something really special has happened to Fen. At least I assume no one else has landed in a zoo. Please speak up if you have."

There was a stunned silence followed by a long, murmured buzzing sound in which the Terran word *zoo,* for which there was no exact Chelan equivalent, could be heard repeated many times. "I thought not," Filya said. "Therefore be quiet and listen to Fen."

Like many another temporarily paralyzed speaker, Fen turned to his most interesting prop for assistance. Scrabble was awake and willing, at least for the moment, to be held and stroked without being fed. "This is one of four fennec fox kits that were born a week ago in the quarters of my Terran sister, Daria Wells," he began. "She is my special pet, but only one of almost fifty animals, not counting the wild water birds I hope you can see on the pond, that are kept on my family's estate."

There was a collective sigh of astonishment and longing, and a wave of green, tinged here and there with yellow, swept over the bodies of his listeners. Fen had his audience in thrall. And once he started, it was easy to talk on and on. After he had described the animals he lived with and saw every day, he went on to tell about the Hudson Valley Ark and his friendship with Giovanna Ferrante, concluding with a detailed description of the gene bank and the wonders it contained.

Filya had not heard this last and most startling piece of news, and Fen had to admire the aplomb with which she pretended to know all about it while bringing her fellow Chelans to order and requiring them to question him one at a time. Binya, her hands buried in her horse's mane, her golden eyes blazing in her dark green face, summed up the babbling of the Group. "This is wonderful news," Binya declared. "It means that all we have to do is decide what animals we want and carry off samples of their DNA."

Even though his own mind had been running on exactly the same track, Fen was appalled at her words and at the enthusiasm they aroused in her listeners. "It would be hideously complicated," he cried. "You have no idea. The place is almost impossible to get into, and then you would need hours and hours of computer time. There are hundreds of thousands, probably millions, of samples. Don't even think of it."

"How can we not think of it?" Tendron growled. "It is the obvious answer. I can't be the only one who has been wondering how to get even one pair of animals back to

Chela, and with only one there would be too little genetic diversity."

"To put it mildly," Fen mumbled. He was wondering what had possessed him to share the secret of the gene bank with the Group. Where would it all end? It was only too easy to guess and to imagine himself (with what, a shopping bag?) prowling the freezing corridors of the gene bank and jumping at every sound. "The whole idea needs a lot of work," he said, and was not reassured by the hearty laughter of his friends.

"We rely on you, dear Fen. I confess I was frantic thinking about how large my beloved horses are and how unlikely they are to have more than one or at the most two offspring." Binya laid her lovely green face against the glossy neck of her mount and gazed appealingly at Fen, who was scanning the faces of the other seven in the vain hope of seeing a flicker of doubt to match his own.

"We must be sure to have ferrets," called Idron from his farmhouse in the south of France. Idron's ferret, who was draped around his neck, nibbled his ear. "They are very engaging animals, and rodents are among their favorite foods, so we won't have to worry about feeding them."

"And birds—all kinds of birds." This was Melinya, who was standing in a tropical garden with a yellow bird on each shoulder. "They eat insects, so they are ideal for us."

"I know," Fen said glumly. "Some do; some don't. Some eat seeds, some fruit. Some must have small, live mammals, others fish, and still others the flesh of many and various dead creatures. You can't just blithely say, 'We must have birds,' Melinya. I'm sorry. I didn't mean to pick on you." Melinya, the youngest of the Group, was hanging her head and looking crestfallen.

"Obviously each of us should make a list." This was the voice of Filya, bossy, managerial, and extremely welcome to Fen. He hoped that making lists would take some time.

"Make lists," he urged his friends. "Make long and detailed lists, including, please, the Latin name of each animal, which I must have to query the computer. Try to think beyond your own dear pets and find out what is unique to your region. Try to think about ecological balance, about predator and prey, about climate and food sources, about at least a million things that none of us has thought about before. I, in the meantime, will add to my other problems the question of breaking and entering as applied to one of the most secure facilities I have ever seen. Wish me luck."

"We do, we do," they cried, their amber eyes glowing, feverish with hope and anticipation.

"Someone is entering your space, Fen," said Filya. "This is unfortunate. We had many more questions to ask you."

"How do you know?" Fen asked, but then he, too, heard the footsteps and the merry, tuneless whistling of Roger Wells. He was saved from a tidal wave of difficult questions, but he also was bitterly disappointed. They had agreed that no Terran would be allowed to see them in communication with each other, but now this seemed a stupid and arbitrary rule. One by one his friends were calling goodbye and fading from the screen, leaving an ache of loneliness. I wanted to chat, Fen thought, not discuss, not plan—just chat. I wanted to know why Binya had a horse to ride and what Idron fed his ferret, whether anyone else had been swimming or had eaten hamburgers.

The last to go was, of course, Filya. "I'll call you later," she said. "We have much to discuss."

"I won't be home," Fen growled, and made a dive on his hands and knees for the monitor screen, which he managed to cover with leaf mold before Roger came through the bushes behind him.

"Lost something?" Roger asked.

"Scrabble was trying to get away," Fen improvised hastily, which was not far from the truth, since the tiny fox had almost been buried with the monitor screen. She was whimpering now against his chest and working her way up, he suspected, to a full display of infant anguish.

"She seems to be thriving, if strength of vocalization is any clue."

"She's fine but always hungry, so we must be off to the milk supply." Fond as he was of Roger, Fen was not in a mood to chat with anyone but his Chelan friends.

"Don't let me detain you for even a moment," Roger said, as Scrabble's complaint grew in volume and complexity.

Fen trudged down toward the house while Roger continued on along the edge of the trees. Fen would have to come back before dark to retrieve the monitor, hoping it would return to a reasonable size without too much squeezing and poking. Large or small, a perfect square or a misshapen mess, it had better be available when Filya called.

Fen sighed. Filya would want to help him make a plan

to steal animal genetic material from the banks of the Hudson Valley Ark, and the more he thought about it, the more impossible it seemed. He felt abysmally ignorant, totally unprepared. In the brief exchange with the Group, he had become aware for the first time of something none of them had ever thought about, and that was the problem of choice. Even after revelling in the vast riches of the Ark and then seeing them multiplied thousands of times in the gene bank, it had not occurred to him to ask himself the simple but terrifying question, If I could have whatever I wanted, what would I take? "Think about ecological balance," he had said, "about predator and prey, about climate and food sources." Wise advice to keep his friends at bay while he worried about keys and passwords, exits and entrances, guards and alarms.

Ignoring the sobs of Scrabble, to which he was by now somewhat inured, Fen sat down on a rock halfway between the pond and the house. They had never been directed to abduct any animals, and now he wondered where the idea had come from. From Filya, he thought, with her previous comment that nothing was said "but much was implied." It had been inevitable, he supposed, that each of them, obeying the directive to study the animals of Earth, would be seized by the desire to take some home. In time, however, the impracticality of taking even very small animals back with them would have discouraged even Filya. But then he had seen the gene bank—that treasure-trove of encapsulated animals—and for a moment everything had seemed possible.

Daria came out of the kitchen with a pail of food for the birds, and Fen watched as cranes, geese, and ducks crowded around the slender dark-haired girl in the warm light of late afternoon. Not for the first time he felt a pang of envy and of longing. I could stay here, he thought, and breed animals myself or help Daria or become a keeper at the Ark. Probably all of us could, one way or another. They need so much help, and we would be so good at it. But then the memory of beautiful, bereft Chela struck him with such force that he leaped to his feet with a cry of pain and rushed into the house.

# seventeen

"What lovely handwriting," said Gloria Wells, bending over Fen's shoulder and staring down at the paper in front of him. "That's Chelan script, I suppose. I don't know that I've ever seen any before." Fen looked up from his work and favored Gloria with one of his toothier smiles. He was fond of Mom, but, like everyone else in the family except Roger, he vastly underestimated her intelligence.

"We write very little," he said, "even on keyboards. Mostly we just think at our computers, and they think back at us. I'm sorry. The concept is clumsily expressed. Anyway, Chelan machines are required for this, and none of us brought one. The idea was to throw ourselves entirely upon the technology of Earth. No doubt a good idea, but now that I want to make a few personal notes to myself, I must practice this antique art, which all of us were taught but never expected to use."

Gloria laughed and pulled up a chair. It was the morning after the conference call, and also after his last private conversation with Filya, who had made it clear that he was the only one in a position to make a list of animals for Chela. The rest of the Group would naturally want to contribute, but it was Fen with his huge zoological resources who must produce the master list. Soon—like yesterday. In search of peace and inspiration, he had taken paper and pen to this small table at the edge of the garden and begun laboriously to write. Gloria tucked her small, gold-sandaled feet beneath her on the chair and leaned her elbows on the table.

"I think it delightful that the idea of penmanship as a virtue has not only survived more than a century of technology on Earth but has crossed interstellar space as well," she said. "We have it, too, you know. When I was a little girl, I was made to write and write and write by hand with my lovely voice-activated computer sitting there right at my elbow. It made me very cross."

"Well, now you know why," Fen said. "You might be on a field expedition somewhere without your compupad and have to write something down."

Gloria wrinkled her nose. "You mean like in a jungle or some such hideously uncomfortable place? Not for me, my dear. I leave that sort of thing to my youngest daughter, who would sell her soul to be up to her neck in mud in the path of a charging rhinoceros. To each her own. Anyway, I write only fiction, and exceptionally fictional fiction at that."

"I keep hoping you will let me read some," Fen said politely. Perhaps she would go in search of a manuscript and give him a few minutes to himself.

"*View* some would be more like it," Gloria said. "I'm not altogether sure the consumers of my fiction could read a book if they were stranded with one on a desert island. But please, be my guest. There's a whole stack of them by the living room monitor. You will probably find them very strange."

Fen gave her another, not quite so friendly smile and looked back down at his paper in the hope that he would be spared elaboration. His experience with writers was limited.

"Strange but not without interest," Gloria continued happily. "Nearly everyone, you know, puts down romantic fiction as intellectual trash, but why, one wonders, does it have such vast appeal? What universal well of dreams is tapped when man and woman meet at the prow of a moonlit ship sailing under cover of darkness in dangerous waters?"

Fen stared at his interlocutor. Did this really call for an answer, or was it what these people called a rhetorical question? "I don't know," he said.

Gloria leaned across the table and tapped him lightly on the chest. "Sex," she said. "The dream is sex."

"Ah," said Fen.

"Ah, indeed," said Gloria. "I have been wondering, as a matter of fact, ever since you arrived, whether it would be even remotely plausible to contrive an interplanetary love story. I mean, it has been done before ad nauseam, but only in the realm of fantasy. This, in a certain sense—now that we know some Chelans—would be the real thing. What do you think?"

"What do *I* think?" Fen was trying, without notable success, to control the purple flood that was threatening to overwhelm the stern, cool grey with which he had turned to his intellectual task. "I doubt that interspecies sex between aliens is any more likely to yield viable offspring than it is between Terran animals."

"Dear Fen, I fear you know more about biology than about literature. Nothing needs to actually happen, you know, to make a warm, wonderful, tear-jerking romance. But the attraction must be there. How do you feel, for example, when you see Lily? Here she comes, so talk fast."

Fen looked toward the house, saw Lily coming their way, and hoped that salvation was at hand. "Of course, I find Lily attractive," he said, "and you as well, dear Mom."

It was Gloria's turn to blush, but Lily was upon them before she could think of a response. "Mother love," said Lily, ignoring Fen and perching on the edge of the table with her back to him, "have you seen my brown suede bag? I could swear I left it in the living room day before yesterday. I was wearing my beige tunic that day, and I remember carrying the brown bag because I didn't have time to change things to the cream silk pouch. Anyway, now I really need it for the cinnamon shantung, and I don't see it anywhere."

"Sorry, darling. I thought I saw it there, too, but just out of the corner of my eye, and who knows when. Maybe Fen saw it. Lily, don't sit like that with your back to Fen. You didn't even say good morning."

"Good morning," Lily said, swiveling on the table. From this vantage point it was inevitable that she should see the brown pouch in Fen's lap, especially since it had at that moment begun to move. Small, piteous sounds issued from the opening at the top. "My bag!" Lily screeched. "You took my bag, you unspeakable creep, and put some horrible animal in it."

Scrabble began to squeak and thrust her tiny blind face out between the drawstrings of the bag, which Fen loosened so she could climb up his chest to the hollow of his neck. "It's just a baby fox," he said, "and now you've given her a terrible fright."

"I can't believe it," Lily said. "First you steal my purse, and then you make it into an animal nest. Even Daria would know better."

"Daria may not have much in common with you," Gloria pointed out, "but she does come from the same planet. We must help Fen to understand our customs and feelings, and screaming at him when he makes a mistake is not helpful."

"Mistake, my ass," Lily said. "He saw what he wanted for his smelly little beast, and he took it."

Fen rose with dignity. "Except for her stupid remarks about my beautiful baby fox, there is something in what she says, dear Mom, so do not disturb yourself. As you know, we Chelans are less attached to possessions than you. And now I really must find a quiet place to write. If you want your bag, Lily, you can find me a replacement for it. Scrabble isn't particular."

"Do you have any idea what fox piss does to suede?"

"I'm beginning to," Fen said, and sprinted for the house before Lily could find something to throw.

Back in his room with the door closed, he gave a sigh of relief. What had possessed him to attempt so difficult a task out-of-doors, where he would be prey to a hundred distractions? And besides, inside he had access to the Net and its huge storehouse of fact, theory, speculation, and experiment. By Terran standards Fen was terrifyingly competent in the acquisition and storage of information. That he was often at a loss when it came to using what he had acquired did not make his abilities any less remarkable.

He decided now to make a swift survey of what was known of the ecology of Earth's tropical and warm-temperate zones—the band that most nearly resembled the habitable portions of his home planet. Pulling a box of chocolate cookies close to his elbow, he flung himself at the mountain of data. Hours passed. Scrabble woke again and demanded to be fed, which Fen accomplished without taking his eyes off the screen. Peru pressed his soft nose against the window and then ambled off to trim the grass along the flower beds. At last Fen turned off the computer and sat back with a groan. He knew now how unbelievably intricate were the relationships of the plants and animals of Earth, from bacteria to whales, from molds to giant redwoods. He was even further from knowing what he should select from the gene bank in the unlikely event that he was able to select anything at all.

A hopeful glance at the cookie box showed that at some point he had reached the bottom. "Naptime," Fen muttered, and threw himself down on the bed. Squealing happily, Scrabble rushed to the crook of his neck and buried her cold nose in his ear. While well nourished in his Terran home, Fen had never been able to get enough sleep. If it wasn't one thing, it was another, and now it was his beloved fox kit, who made every nap an event staged entirely for her enjoyment. "Please, Scrabble," Fen said, and Scrabble began to lick his face enthusiastically.

Jumping to his feet, he staggered down the hall to Daria's room. Possibly he could get her to baby-sit for half an hour, although it was hard to imagine how, since Daria had made it abundantly clear that, while the joys of raising a baby animal were to be his alone, so too were the sorrows. After it was too late to retreat, he saw that Daria was cleaning the floor of the aviary and the mongooses' toilet mound. "Welcome, oh animal lover from outer space," Daria cried. "You'll find an extra bucket and scoop leaning against the baobab tree."

"Daria, I'm exhausted."

"Who isn't? Come on, Fen. I'm way behind, and we're supposed to have a major storm tonight, so I have a lot of outside work, too. Park your fox and pick up some poop like a good fellow."

"You don't leave a person a lot of choice, do you?" Fen grumbled, but he joined her in the aviary and took up the slotted scoop with which the endless task of sifting the guano out of the sand and leaf mold on the aviary floor was done. The mongooses were sitting up on the pinnacles of their termite mound watching every move with their bright black eyes. Fen was fond of the mongooses. They were not particularly tame, having a large extended family to relate to, but they always looked as if they would be fun to know. "Nice of these little folks to do it all in one place," he remarked.

"They're good guys," Daria said. "I just have them because I like them, you know, and because I can learn a lot from studying their social behavior, but they're not in the least endangered. Tough as old shoe leather. They like their little African desert because it's like home, but I suspect they could survive almost anywhere."

Fen looked at the mongooses with new interest. Probably they would thrive on Chela, gobbling up insects and small rodents. There was even a Chelan equivalent of a termite mound. He would put them at the head of his list, on the theory that he had to start somewhere. One thing, he supposed, might lead to another, but it was all too complicated to think about now.

Daria straightened her back and gazed up into the branches where the birds were hopping nervously from one perch to another. "They know a storm is coming," she said. "Come on, Fen. We'll call this done for now and go outside. I want to clear out the shed so the llamas will have someplace to shelter."

Fen picked up Scrabble, who was asleep in her pouch, and trailed behind Daria, thinking he would just slip into his room and not come out. This moment of peace was too good to waste, but Daria stopped suddenly in front of the binturongs' cage, and he nearly ran into her. Saskia was in her nest box, looking down at Igor and snarling quietly. "She's about to give birth," Daria said. "I know it. I feel it in my bones."

"Maybe she has already. They could be there in the box."

"Good point. They could be. I just don't think so, somehow."

"Want me to go in and peek?" Fen was not only much taller than Daria, he also had the curious ability to be close to animals without disturbing them, a gift that Daria both envied and sometimes exploited.

"Absolutely not," she said. "We're supposed to leave them strictly alone. We can take an obviously abandoned cub away for hand-rearing. Otherwise, it's hands off. Mother binturongs are touchy, and this is Saskia's first. Giovanna says that if all you do is try to count the litter, the mother will sometimes abandon the whole lot, and then you really have your hands full."

"So what do we do?" Fen asked. "Just wait until she brings them out to play? That could be ages."

Daria laughed. "It's not quite that bad. She'll come out, and we'll see her teats are heavy with milk, or we'll hear baby sounds from inside the box. Then in a few days we can look in the box and examine the cubs. Anyway, this is probably as good a time as any for a blessed event. There isn't a thing I can do, and I'm too busy to worry. Come on. Let's get that shed cleared out. Then I might consider letting you have a nap. You're turning a rather unhealthy color."

"I think I may be dying. There will be nasty repercussions."

"I'll take my chances," Daria said unsympathetically. "But here, have some of Saskia's raisins. Fructose and iron."

Fen glared. He would have preferred junk food, but he accepted the offering and gobbled it down. Feeling better in spite of himself, he followed Daria out to the garden and the heavy work of cleaning out the shed.

# eighteen

By late afternoon Daria had done all that seemed possible to secure her animals against the coming storm. She and Fen had cleared out the shed so that the llamas and any birds that wanted to could go inside. Then she had sent Fen to bed. By now, she thought, Scrabble could chew on his ear without keeping him awake.

The setting sun was a malevolent yellow eye sinking into purple clouds. Stepping out for a last look around the garden, she felt a wave of fear in the suffocating stillness of the air. The leaves hung from the trees, stricken and lifeless. She realized now what a noisy place the garden had been—full of the voices of birds and the snorting of llamas; full of rustling, creaking, squawking, splashing, buzzing, clicking, quacking, honking; full, in short, of the sounds of life, which in their absence left behind this frightening void.

The sound of Roger's little car purring into the drive was loud in the silence but welcome. Then there was Roger himself, a comforting figure standing in the middle of the lawn and surveying the scene with a frown. "Scary," he said. "It's supposed to fall short of a hurricane, but there's a nasty feeling in the air. I wonder if I should bother to cook."

"Sandwiches and coffee are traditional," Daria said, "and those we can get from the slots."

Roger peered through the gloom at the high arch of the aviary and at the curves and bulges of the other animal habitats, all plastic, all tough and resilient but still fragile-looking in the ominous light. "Hatches battened down?" he asked softly.

Daria nodded. "Best I can do. I wish now we didn't have any trees around the house, but that would be dreary in the long run."

"They're healthy and strong," Roger said, "and this is by no means our first big storm. I won't bore you again with tales of the storms we had in my youth, but they did make me an architect of sturdy forms. This house has stood up well."

"Even the bubbles," Daria said, "but they still look vulnerable."

"I wouldn't worry. Go in and hold a few paws. The creatures are going to be scared." Roger began to drift by force of habit toward the kitchen.

"They already are." Daria resisted the temptation to follow her father. He was right. Her place was with her animals, but why did she always have to do everything alone?

The house contained a mother, a father, two large siblings, and an alien. Of the lot, the alien was the only one likely to keep her company during the storm, and he might well sleep through the whole thing.

She found the same unnatural stillness in her room, and there, at such close proximity to so many animals, it was even more disquieting. The birds still fluttered nervously, but all the other animals were still, and many were invisible, tucked into their dens. Daria pictured the large tamarin family inside its hollow tree and envied them their closeness. The mongooses were in their termite mound, the turtles in their shells. Even the snakes had found dark corners in which to coil. Poor Igor, perhaps feeling that the palm frond nest was too exposed, had curled into a tight ball under an overhanging rock at the back of the cage while Saskia occupied the nesting box.

"This is what I get for not having a pet," Daria mumbled. "A nice dog would be right in my lap, panting and slobbering and making me feel needed." She considered getting into her own nest up in the loft and pulling the covers over her head, but instead she sat in the big swivel chair.

The storm came all at once with the shriek of a banshee from hell. Trees that had stood without the quiver of a leaf in the lifeless air writhed and lashed against a nearly black sky. The fact that the trees inside the animal habitats were almost still made the torment of those outside all the more terrifying.

Daria huddled with her hands over her ears to muffle

the inhuman screaming of the gale and the frightened cries of the birds. It was almost dark, and the lights that normally came on automatically at dusk did not come on. At first there had been no rain, but now it burst upon the plastic domes in a torrent, adding the thunder of falling water to the howling wind.

"Poor Saskia," Daria said. "I'll have to see if she needs help, rules or no rules." Saskia and Igor were wild animals, and Daria had tried to keep it that way. But they also were accustomed to her voice and looked to her for food. They nuzzled her when she went into their cage and followed her around while she hid their snacks. Perhaps Saskia would find her keeper a comfort if she was giving birth in a terrible storm.

Since the main power was obviously off, Daria switched on the emergency generator, and the harsh light flared in the binturong habitat, leaving pools of black shadow. She was just in time to see Saskia start down the tree that held her nest box. Her eyes glittered with fear in the sudden illumination, and her claws scrabbled on the bark. When she reached the bottom, she ran for the darkest corner, leaving a trail of fluid behind her on the bare floor, and there she turned on Daria and snarled. Not knowing what else to do, Daria crouched by the entrance flap, calling what she hoped were reassuring endearments over the raging of the storm. In spite of the emergency light, she could barely see the animal, who had backed under a mat of low, leafy branches, but it seemed certain that she was having her babies.

"Why didn't you stay in your box, silly beast?" Daria said. "Why come out in the open? What kind of sense does that make, and what did I do to deserve this?" The storm seemed to be worsening, and Daria saw to her horror that things were starting to fly past the house—first just small branches and leaves, then much larger things such as bicycles and garbage cans. A huge limb from the oak in the middle of the garden crashed to the ground inches from the plastic shell that separated the animals from the raging world outside, and a terrified mother binturong ran screaming up into her nesting box. If babies had been born in the dark corner of the cage, they had been left behind.

Cursing and crying, Daria scrambled out of the cage and started pulling everything out of the drawers in the big table. Somewhere she had a sort of miner's light that she could wear on her head. She found it finally and ran back to the cage. There were four newborn binturongs squirming under the canopy of leaves. Even covered with blood and amniotic fluid and with their eyes shut tight, they looked like miniature editions of their parents. All but one were about eight inches long with tails almost as long again. All but one were mewing pitifully. The fourth cub was very small, not much more than half the size of its siblings, and its cries were barely audible. "You'll never make it, poor baby," Daria said, "but neither will the rest of the crew unless I do something pretty fast. Will Saskia take them back, if I put them up there? Is it even possible? Is it worth a try?"

She picked up the biggest and most rambunctious baby, the one most likely to appeal to an unsentimental animal mother. At this point she realized that she couldn't reach the nest box without a stepladder. With a whimper of frustration, Daria stepped back and straight into the arms of Fen, who had appeared under cover of the storm and now stood right behind her.

"Let me try," Fen said, and Daria handed him the little animal.

She stood back, aware that she was trembling, aware, too, that the storm had blown itself out and was now no more than rain and gusting wind. What rotten luck—if only Saskia could have waited. But Daria supposed fear had brought her labor on. "It won't work, you know," she said to Fen. "There's no way she's going to accept those babies after what she's been through."

"I know only one way to find out," said Fen. His voice was serene and far away, all his senses concentrated on the dark nesting box and its frightened occupant.

"Do you want my light?" Daria whispered, but he merely shook his head. He had slipped the baby into the box with one long hand, and now he waited, making a low humming noise, his skin a dark but curiously luminous green. "Give me another," Fen said finally. "Give me the tiny one."

"Let's save the big ones," Daria said, and was surprised that he did not argue but took the baby she handed him and went through the same process as before.

"She's cleaning them," Fen reported in a low voice, "and the first has begun to suckle. Wait a minute. Yes, there goes number two. Slurp, slurp. Give me number three."

When Daria had given Fen the third baby to introduce to its mother, she picked up the runt and held it close. She thought its chances among its three rugged siblings would be slim. "Let's hand-rear this one," she said when Fen turned around for the last time. "It'll never make it without help and probably not then. Could you find me a damp rag, some disinfectant, and a bit of Scrabble's milk?"

An hour later they sat together in the middle of Daria's room, listening to the storm rumble away toward the coast and watching the runt binturong sleep in Daria's lap. It had been cleaned up, had the stump of umbilical cord disinfected, and taken a few drops of milk. Daria still thought little of its chances but was satisfied, since Fen reported mother and babies happily asleep in their box.

"Without you, they would all have died," Daria said.

Fen shrugged. "You would have hand-reared at least some of them, but what a job. I could imagine myself feeding baby binturongs around the clock. It was a matter of self-preservation."

Daria laughed. "It was not."

"It absolutely was."

"Well, I wish I knew your secret. You don't even have much experience with animals, but they grow calm when you're near as if you've waved a magic wand."

"There is no magic," Fen said. "I am tall, and I have better night vision than you, so I could sort of see what was going on in the box. The flashlight might have been traumatic. Who knows? Anyway, I was able to work without it."

Daria continued to stare at her alien assistant. On the whole, she thought, he was right. There was no mystery in his way with animals. Probably, and this was rather sad, the biggest thing Fen had going for him was that he was not human. Whatever he smelled of, there was no scent to arouse the old ancestral fear. He was not human, and he was unclassifiable as predator or prey. He was simply himself—a totally unthreatening entity. Still, there was a little more to it than that—the almost frightening concentration and, above all, the empathy that she thought surpassed that of the most gifted animal handler she had ever known.

They sat through the night, taking turns holding the tiny animal, feeding it a few drops of milk, stroking it, keeping it warm. Its response was very feeble, and twice Daria thought it had slipped away, but when the first watery rays of sunlight slanted through the drenched trees, it was still alive.

"You look closer to death than the little one," Daria said to Fen. "Why not go and pass out for a few hours? I'm okay for now." It was her turn to hold the baby, and Fen seemed to be asleep sitting up.

He opened one eye, groaned, and closed it again. "Scrabble," he said, "must be screaming by now. Left her in bed. Have to feed."

"Bring her here," Daria said. "I can put this one down

while I give Scrabble a snack. Then she can go back in her pouch and yell or sleep for all I care. Get some rest, Fen. I'm going to need you."

"You are a true friend," Fen said, and staggered off to do as he had been told.

# nineteen

"Busy, busy, busy," Fen said. He was talking to Filya, who had caught him dashing to one of the new baby's innumerable feedings. Daria was out. Fen was late. And here was Filya. It was ever thus. "Let me call you back."

"You won't."

"I will. I'll call you from Daria's room. What do you think of that?"

"Too good to be true."

"Don't go away," Fen said, and flipped her off.

When the little binturong had been fed and tucked in his box, Fen made good on his promise and even toured the animal enclosures with the monitor so that Filya could at last see what he had been talking about.

"You deserve this," he said, "but truly it has been very rare for Daria to be gone in any way I could count on. Soon it will be no problem, since she will be in school all day, but so, I suppose, will you."

"How can I even think of school in the presence of all these animals?" Filya's eyes were dilated, and her skin flooded with various shades of green. "But yes. Yes, I am about to go to school. I expect it will bore me out of my mind, but at least I will get out of the house. Oh, the mongooses are dear. Fen, I want some."

"I, on the other hand," said Fen, trying not to sound smug, "have been reprieved."

"Reprieved from what—from school?"

"I am to be a volunteer at the Ark and help Giovanna Ferrante. When I told her I didn't want to go to school, she interceded for me with the family, and what could they say? Daria, of course, is wild with jealousy, but at least I will be able to help her out, since my hours at the Ark are shorter than hers at school."

"It's not fair," Filya said.

"What's not fair?"

"Why should you have all the luck?"

"I don't know," Fen said. "It's just a matter of where I landed, Filya. I can't help it. When you get to feeling really abused, you can think about how tired I am all the time, and it can only get worse. I am trying to do without naps, but we don't seem to be made that way. At least they are getting shorter all the time. Once in a while I fall asleep on my feet."

"I wish I could sympathize," Filya said. Her joyful

greens were definitely yellowing now. "Why are you more tired than before?"

"We have a new baby animal to hand-rear. He is very fragile and needs to be fed every two hours and held a lot, and Scrabble hasn't exactly grown up in the interval."

"I don't want to hear about it," Filya said. "What I want to hear is that you have completed the list of genetic material to be taken from the Ark. Tendron, by the way, has undertaken to learn genetic engineering, so when we have acquired the samples, we will know what to do with them."

"He's what?" Fen spluttered. "Filya, have you all gone mad? Tendron is brilliant, but he only heard of DNA about a week ago. Generations of Earth scientists have been working on this problem, and even now they say they can't create a whole species, so what is poor Tendron supposed to do?"

"He will be a resource."

"A resource," Fen repeated.

"Fen, we have scientists who can run rings around anyone on Earth, and you know it. Think of U-Bandor, for example."

"But not in zoology," Fen said gloomily.

"I don't understand why you are so negative," Filya said. "You act as if you have given up, and that worries me, since you are the only one in a position to do the job."

"I haven't given up. Why do you think I wangled this position at the Ark?"

"So you could have more fun with animals."

Like all half-truths, this was infuriating. "You're being tedious, and I am bored," Fen said. "We will talk again when you have something useful to say."

Filya's shriek of rage was easy to cut short, but having done so, he couldn't help feeling guilty—not guilty enough to call back, but guilty just the same. He took the infant binturong out of his box and let him snuggle in his hand. Against Fen's chest the fox kit slumbered in her pouch. Slowly Fen lowered himself into Daria's big chair and tried to focus on the problems he was supposed to solve. "One," he muttered, "make ecologically correct list of several hundred hardy tropical animals. Two, figure out how to steal, preserve, and transport their genetic material to Chela. Three, figure out how to train Chelan scientists to make many, many animals out of a few snippets of DNA. Four, take long nap here in nice chair before Daria comes home."

When Daria arrived, hot and cross from a day of tests and counseling, she found him sprawled in her chair and blissfully asleep, an infant binturong on his stomach, a fox kit just beginning to stir in the pouch on his chest. Tenderness at this lovely sight mingled with exasperation as she remembered that he would be at the Ark while she languished in the classroom. She had taken this matter up with Giovanna to absolutely no avail.

"Of course I could get you out of school, *cara mia.* For me this is child's play. But I will not do it. You must mingle with other young people. You must have a life that is not of the zoo."

Daria had argued that she didn't like the teenagers she met at school, that they didn't like her, and that there were young people only slightly older than herself working as interns at the Ark. She had reminded Giovanna of her own unconventional youth, to which the inevitable reply had been that Daria should be glad to be spared the conditions under which Giovanna had grown up.

Resisting the temptation to drop her notebook on Fen's head, Daria started to turn away but stopped as a strange object caught her eye. In Fen's left hand was what Daria instinctively felt to be a completely alien object, even though it closely resembled a child's sketching board—the kind you drew on by turning two little knobs and could erase by pulling up a piece of plastic. It was grey and about six inches square. Next to it was a tiny instrument shaped like a morning glory.

As Daria stared, the pouch on Fen's chest gave a convulsive leap, followed shortly by the emergence of Scrabble. Digging her claws in to gain purchase on the smooth lavender skin of her surrogate mother, the tiny fox made her unsteady way to his chin and began to lick. Fen jumped and made a grab for Scrabble, which caused him to drop the communicator. Daria picked it up.

"Hi," Daria said. "What's this?" She felt a little sorry for Fen, who seemed to be struck dumb. He held out his hand, and she put the two alien objects into it.

"It's a communicator," he said finally. "I don't know why you shouldn't know. It's just that we were taught to keep these things a secret and not to let you people know that we could communicate with each other."

"I think that's neat," Daria said. "And it makes sense. You must be lonely scattered all over the globe the way you are. Show me how it works."

Fen turned dark purple. "I can't do that," he said. "It's frightfully taboo. If I showed you another Chelan, I would be severely reprimanded for telling you about it."

"That's silly—unless you guys are plotting to overthrow the world government or something."

"Good joke," Fen said. "Not really. Here, have a baby animal. I seem to have more than I need. Take Billy. It must be almost time for him to eat."

Well aware that she was being put off, Daria picked up the baby binturong and cuddled him briefly before putting him back in his box. He was still asleep, and she was not about to wake him up to find out if he was hungry. That would be made all too clear, all too soon. "I guess you'll have to take both babies to the Ark when you go," she said. "I don't know. This never came up before. Going to school and taking care of the animals just always meant a lot more work; I was never hand-rearing anything."

"I could do that," Fen said, "though I suspect two baby animals would greatly interfere with my work, not to mention all that I want to learn. Maybe I could get Mom to feed them while I'm gone."

"You have to be kidding."

"No, why? She is always here. I know she works on her stories, but she could take a few minutes off from time to time."

"Interrupting Mom at her work is like interrupting a lioness at her kill. Not recommended."

"We won't be around to be savaged," Fen said cheerfully. "If she agrees in principle, I'll put a reminder on her computer. She wouldn't let a baby animal starve."

"Want to bet?"

Fen stuffed the communicator into Scrabble's pouch, settled Scrabble on his neck, and heaved himself out of the chair. "I shall ask," he said. "Wish me luck."

"I do, I do." Daria watched him go, adding, "Or do I?" once he was out the door. It occurred to her that he would probably succeed where she would almost certainly have failed. Although that was unfair, the notion that her mother might be converted to an even occasional animal feeder was so bizarre and delightful that it was impossible not to hope for his success. In a better mood than she had been in all day, Daria kicked off her school shoes and began her evening chores.

# twenty

So began a summer that Fen would spend in a daze of happiness. True, he was tired a good deal of the time and also hot, for even a Chelan could not fail to be affected by the temperatures on an average July afternoon in the Hudson Valley during the late twenty-first century. The growing frequency with which his friends, usually by way of Filya, but sometimes in groups of three or four or even eight, reminded him of his responsibilities to the Group might also have dimmed the bliss with which he woke each morning or tormented the sleep into which he sank with a happy sigh each night, but such was not the case. For Fen, at home and at work, was wallowing in animals, and this was the greatest joy he had ever known.

Roger taught him to drive and lent him the family's smallest car for his trips to the Ark. The car, which was red, had a sun roof, and Fen drove with the seat pushed all the way back and his head sticking out the top. For a few days everyone at the Ark who could manage it lined up at the parking lot to view his arrival. Several minor accidents were reported from the freeway.

His work for Giovanna did not consist, as he had thought it would, in the kind of dung-shoveling, floor-scrubbing activities that occupied the interns. Had he not been an alien, there might have been hard feelings, for Giovanna had a list of ethology and animal communication projects as long as her arm, and Fen was put to work on them. These were things that Giovanna had always wanted to know, such as what alligators said to each other underwater and would a hammerhead stork prefer bones and scraps of hide to more attractive man-made materials to decorate the top of its nest. Most of these projects, though prestigious from the standpoint of the apprentices, were less than thrilling and involved many hours of observation. To Fen they were consistently fascinating.

He was particularly enchanted by the elegant brown storks, which seemed to devote their lives to the construction of a truly enormous nest. The pair Fen was studying was almost finished with a structure that was six feet tall and might weigh more than two hundred pounds. The heavy work being done, it was now time to decorate the roof, and to this end the ornithologists at the Ark had provided a varied and changing assortment of materials for the birds to choose from.

"And choose is what they do," the curator said to Fen.

"What we want to know is what's going on in those funny, hammer-shaped heads while they're doing it."

Animal cognition had seized the imagination of zoologists shortly before the turn of the century and then been buried in the more urgent problems associated with simply keeping the animals alive through the violent climate changes of the environmental crash. Now, in the quiet aftermath, it was more than ever the subject of intense thought and research, as if in recognizing the common peril, man had at last come to understand his kinship with animals.

Thus Fen was involved in tabulating a bewildering matrix of choice and rejection. He was given a list of the goodies of the day—dried snakeskins, used tea bags, glowing peacock feathers, bedraggled chicken feathers, buttons, gnawed bones, to name only a few—and set to recording what the birds did with them. That Fen never seemed to tire of this sort of thing made him a celebrity around the Ark and much in demand.

"He's an ethology machine," Giovanna said one night when she and Daria were talking over the computer link. "I wish I could clone him. Now, mind you, I've sat in a Land Rover all day at a hundred and ten in the shade for weeks on end to watch some critters go about their daily rounds and been happy as a loon, but that would be my own research project, not a little piece of someone else's."

"I know," Daria said. "It's weird. He's weird. You know, I guess, that he persuaded my mom to feed the baby animals when he's not home and taught her how to do it."

"Yes, I know, and it scares me out of my wits. No offense, *cara,* but your mother is a flitterywidget."

"That's not quite right," Daria said, laughing, "but now I'll never think how the silly word does go. Yes, she is, though Fen doesn't think so. I'll leave the channel open so you or someone can peek from time to time. Don't worry about the baby fox. She is brokenhearted when Fen leaves and beside herself with joy when he comes home, but she still eats, and soon she will have her eyes open and be getting into everything."

In his spare time Fen roamed the wide precincts of the Ark, from the dappled woodlands where otters romped and wolves lay panting in the shade to sunbaked rocks and dusty wallows, from tigers to mice to crocodiles. When, after many promises had been broken, it became clear that he would not stay out of the enclosures where dangerous animals were housed, he was lent one of the little cars the Ark people used in the hope that this would deter all but the most infuriated large animal from doing him harm.

Fen wandered and observed and filed things away in his capacious brain. The reproaches of his fellow Chelans were unfounded, for Fen was working on his list. But he had learned a lesson from the first conference call about getting their hopes up and letting their imaginations run riot. The most he would say was that his position at the Ark was bound to come in handy, and only time would tell how this might happen.

Increasingly aware of the obstacles to his friends' mad scheme of stealing animal genetic material on Earth and turning it into animals on Chela, he found himself at the same time growing ever more determined to carry it out. He was far from immune to the emotion that had seized Filya at the sight of the dwarf mongooses. They were enchanting, and one wanted to possess them. He wanted to possess every creature he saw, and every creature he saw he could imagine in his distant home.

Sitting in one of the great tropical aviaries at the end of a steamy afternoon, he would feel it quietly transformed into a Chelan glade. And slowly, as if painting with his mind, he would fill its empty branches with the bright birds of Earth and break its silence with their myriad cries.

To Giovanna, who was doing a little ethology project of her own, the behavior of her newest intern was fascinating, as were the questions he asked. Although his work was in animal behavior, his chief interest appeared to be technical ecology. He was preoccupied, for example, with food chains, from top to bottom and in the most excruciating detail.

His continuing interest in the gene bank was also disturbing. It wasn't so much that he found it interesting and used the computer to study its contents. That Giovanna could understand. It was the way she sometimes found him just standing there in one of the corridors, staring at the rows of little drawers with those glowing yellow eyes. "It means something special to him," Giovanna said to Daria. "Something heavy and fraught with an emotion that I can't begin to imagine."

At the end of June a shipment of tiger sperm arrived from Antwerp, and the container was added to a pile already standing in the hall, thus drawing Fen's attention to what appeared to be a collection of high-tech picnic hampers.

"These are awesome," the young technician said in response to Fen's studiously casual question. "So much better than we used to have—stay cold almost indefinitely. Not that more than a few days is usually needed, but still, it's nice to know you've got the extra time when something major is being moved."

"What do you mean by almost indefinitely? Weeks? Months? Years?" Fen had become adjusted to human hyperbole.

"I mean minus one hundred twenty-two degrees Celsius for at least six months," the technician said. "Beyond that no one has bothered to test."

The following day one of the containers disappeared, but it was not actually missed for several weeks, at which point a search was made and then abandoned. It became one of those mysteries that plague all organizations from families to vast corporations. Things, even quite large things, slip between the floorboards and seldom come back up. The search had not extended to an overgrown and unused burrow in the wolf woods.

Fen's day at the Ark was shorter than Daria's at school, and much as he loved his time in the enormous zoo, he was always glad to get home to what he now thought of as his own animals. Scrabble was looking more like a fox all the time. A delicate, creamy fuzz now covered her formerly hairless body, and her ears, which had hung limply on either side of her head, were starting to stiffen and stand up in proper fox fashion. When her eyes opened, she gazed with joy and amazement upon the great world and set out to chew it up. "I can't bear to put her in a cage," Gloria cried, "but what am I to do? I only have two hands. Fen, do something. Those are Daria's best shoes." Gloria was feeding Billy while Scrabble laid waste to everything that was not nailed down.

Fen scooped up his pet and held her, wriggling, in front of his face. Scrabble made a delighted lunge and bit his nose with her tiny needle teeth. "You might try tying her to your chair," he said, "but then she would probably chew on your ankles."

"Think again," Gloria said. She massaged Billy's bottom gently with a damp paper towel until he peed into the paper towels on her lap. "I still can't believe I'm doing this."

"It's maternal instinct. All females have it."

"Maybe that's true where you come from, though frankly you sound to me like a typical adolescent male spouting off about something he knows nothing about. It certainly isn't true here."

Fen shrugged. "Look at yourself. Beautiful, well-dressed professional woman. Children all grown up. Letting a little, bedraggled, ratlike animal pee in your lap."

"Ratlike! Bedraggled! How dare you?" Gloria crushed the tiny binturong to her admirable bosom, and they both laughed.

"I agree he is beautiful," Fen said, "and it appears that he will live—thanks in large part to you."

"Can we ever put him back with his mom? Much as I would miss him, they seem to have such a lovely time."

"I doubt it," Fen said. "Look at the size difference. Even if she agreed, the others would probably make hamburger of him, and she wouldn't even have a nipple for him anymore. You know each one has its own faucet?"

"Its very own?"

"Its very own. Noninterchangeable."

They both stared in at Saskia, who had made a stately descent to the palm frond nest with her lusty triplets on her back and was now engaged in suckling them. Igor, no longer an outcast but not exactly welcome either, gave his family a quick nuzzle and went for a climb in the lower branches.

"I'm beginning to understand what you people see in animals," Gloria said. "Sort of. Don't quote me."

Fen smiled wistfully and wandered off to check the other animals. He was thinking that none of them, even Daria and Giovanna, had any idea what animals meant to him and that this was a lonely state of affairs. The turtle tank needed cleaning—a gigantic job for the end of a tiring day. He looked in at the turtles, and they nudged the glass with their beaky noses, then swerved away again in elegant arcs through their slightly murky water. Fen sighed, grabbed a handful of raisins from the supply table, and turned the valve that would drain the tank.

July was slightly less exhausting, if only because there were fewer bottle feedings. The babies were growing up and needed to be fed only every five or six hours. The other side of the coin was that they grew livelier and, at least in Scrabble's case, more destructive by the minute. Billy was less into chewing and more into climbing. He would climb anything that stood still and some things that didn't, such as people and aliens. He liked to hang by his tail from a person's arm and be swung vigorously to and fro. Lacking a person, he was fond of climbing to the top of the tree in the middle of Daria's room. From there he stared down at his keepers, his merry black eyes glittering below white-fringed ears. Since both young animals now had to stay in cages when there was no one to play with them, this made for a lively morning chase when Daria and Fen were both late for school or work.

This summer idyll was brought to an abrupt end with the shrilling of the communicator in the middle of a stifling August night. Fen had gone to bed early after a wearing day and was in the deepest trough of sleep. His groggy protests died at the sight of Filya's face, which was a dark, muddy ocher. "This is a conference call, Fen," she said without preamble. "Something nasty has happened. Wake up and stretch your screen out while I bring the others in."

In spite of his fright, it was hard to wake up. He sat on the edge of the bed fumbling with the screen and listening to the confused sounds of other Chelan voices as Filya struggled with the controls. When the Group was finally assembled on his monitor, he saw that they were all much the same sickly color. Whatever the news, it was bad, and he was clearly the last to hear it. Binya sat drooping on her horse, Idron held his ferret cradled in his arms, and Melinya stood surrounded by birds with tears pouring down her face. "What is it?" Fen cried. "You all look terrible."

It was Tendron who answered him in a hollow voice. "We've been recalled. We must be at the spaceport two Earth weeks from tonight. We have been advised to travel light."

"I don't understand," Fen said numbly.

"Who does?" Filya snapped. "It's politics. Who understands politics? Or money. Likewise. Personally, I think it's money, although the Powers know now that we're here, we're not costing anyone anything."

"I spoke with U-Bandor myself," Tendron said. "You know how much we mean to him. Our research would have been the crowning achievement of his life, but he said he could do nothing."

Sorrow swept over Fen like a black tide. The pain began with Scrabble—her tiny paws kneading his chest, her small, warm body squirming in the hollow of his neck—and spread to a hundred beloved animals he would never see again. I'll stay, he thought in desperation. They can say I died. The thought was banished almost as soon as it was born. If he betrayed the Group and his homeland, he would never have another happy moment here on Earth.

Binya lifted a tear-streaked face from her horse's mane. "Too bad you couldn't have moved a little faster, Fen. Now we'll have to return without either animals or genetic material, and who knows if we'll ever get to come back."

Fen buried his face in his hands. "I'm not sure," he muttered.

"You're not sure of what, Fen?" Tendron asked in a surprisingly gentle voice.

"I've done more than any of you know. I didn't want to be pestered to get this or that. I wanted to work it all out scientifically, and there's still so much to do. But basically, if I didn't get caught, I could steal a container of DNA samples tomorrow. I'm still not sure what you think you're going to do with this stuff when you get it home, but if this is what you want, I'll try to do it. It will be a suitable gift for U-Bandor. Please don't everyone look so happy. I see nothing to be happy about."

# twenty-one

Roger was driving Daria home from school. They were often short one car these days, and if the twins stayed late at school or left early, Daria had to be picked up.

"He told me he was sleeping over at a friend's house," Daria said, "so not to worry when he didn't come home. I don't know why this sounds so fishy."

"I don't either. He must have made friends at the Ark besides Giovanna. Everyone there is as loony about animals as he is. They'll probably stay up all night trading critter stories."

"I know. It's just that . . . well, it's an old excuse. It reminds me of a twentieth-century book I read where the girl is always telling her mother she's sleeping over with a girlfriend when she's actually sleeping over with a boyfriend. It has that kind of flavor."

“Quaint folks, those twentieth-centurians,” Roger commented.

“Weren’t they? Well, here we are. I’m sure all this means is more work for me,” Daria said, as her father steered into the carport and they both got out.

Far from having a cozy chat with a like-minded young person, Fen was lonely, nervous, and bored, though grateful that he had remembered to bring food. He was spending the late afternoon and evening in the little red car, now well camouflaged with mud and parked in a thicket outside the back entrance to the wolf woods. It was broiling in the car, and after a while it occurred to him to stretch out on the ground and try to sleep. This was an improvement, and though he had thought himself to be a mass of jangling nerves, he was soon asleep.

He woke when an owl called from the woods and lay looking up at the familiar stars of Earth. From the bare knoll above the otter pond, a wolf began to howl and was soon joined by the other members of the pack, the eerie harmonies rising and falling in the warm darkness. I may never hear them again, Fen thought, and felt the sharp pain between his eyes that was a prelude to tears.

Giovanna, primed for a pleasant evening at home, found herself too restless to stay inside. Dinner and wine had produced neither sleepiness nor any inclination to scholarship. “I’ll just walk partway back,” she said to the python on the couch. "I promise not to stay, as if you cared."

In the end she walked much farther than she had meant to. The winding paths of the Ark were dimly lighted by little mushroom lamps. Giovanna could sense the animals on either side—some sleeping on their feet; some curled in dens; some wide-eyed, enlivened by the dark, rustling, leaping, calling in the night. On a rocky hillside a leopard coughed—another of the Ark's outstanding success stories that somehow always reminded Giovanna of another failure. Zoologists had known for a century that they would lose the cheetah, but there had been a period of hope, which only made the ultimate extinction of the world's swiftest cat that much more painful. It had been another ending to which Giovanna had been an unwilling witness. "What a beauty you were," she whispered, remembering the small, poised head with its black stripes, so much like tears, running down from its eyes; the elegant body built for such incredible speed; the long, clean line of the tail. If we can ever bring a species back, she thought, let's start with the cheetah. But there, I'll never live to see that day.

Feeling suddenly tired and even a little old, Giovanna took the path to the main building and sat down at one of the tables in the courtyard. It was late, and the cafeteria was closed, nor did there appear to be anyone working in the labs. Far below, through the heavy summer foliage, she could see the river gleaming faintly in the starlight. The footsteps of the night watchman rang on the flagstones, fading away as he rounded the far end of the North Wing, and still Giovanna sat, enjoying the quiet, wrapped in her thoughts.

Like a thin slice of fog, Fen slipped around the South Wing and into the shadow of the portico. He had timed the passage of the guard to give him five minutes at the door, which was about four minutes longer than he needed to penetrate its already well-studied codes. Perhaps if he had seen Giovanna, he might have panicked and thrown the whole enterprise to the wind, but sitting in the dark against a background of trees, she was nearly as invisible as he. The lock yielded in seconds, and he was inside, turning in the faint blue light down the familiar corridor to the cold banks of drawers he knew so well.

The computer hummed quietly in its alcove, working unattended through the night. Swiftly Fen entered the codes that gave him access to the gene bank. Then for a long moment he stood, holding the amulet in the hollow of his joined hands. A deep breath; an act of will. *"Felidae,"* Fen whispered. *"Neofelis, nebulosa."* Off to his left an arrow flashed. Seizing his hamper of liquid nitrogen, he strode to the home of the clouded leopard.

He worked as fast as he dared, with the deep concentration that was one of the glories of his race. He thought it would take all that was left of the night to fill the abbreviated list he had made with so much anguish during the last three days. Time was strictly limited; he would need to be gone before first light.

A whisper of sound, an almost imperceptible shift in the cold, dense air, and he froze with his hand on the drawer that held the genetic plan of the American alligator. Someone had entered the dim labyrinth of the gene bank almost as silently as he had and was now watching him. With racing heart Fen whirled to confront the intruder. His skin was black, his eyes almost red in the near-darkness. Intending to frighten the watchman and run with what he had, Fen was totally unprepared for the sight of Giovanna Ferrante. He gave a cry of despair and dropped to his knees. Short of the truth, there was no explanation, and telling the truth was more than he could even contemplate.

At last, though not without difficulty of her own, the director of the Ark spoke to the alien thief of genes. "Pick up your case, Fen, and come along," she said. "We're going to raid the kitchen."

"Giovanna, please, just let me go home. Forget you saw me. Think of it as a bad dream," Fen babbled, but followed the tall woman down the hall toward the cafeteria.

"Ha," Giovanna said over her shoulder, "what a hope." And that was all she said until she had unlocked the cafeteria and provisioned them with a box of cookies and a bottle of local wine.

The next thing she said was, "Don't even think of it. You wouldn't get far, and it would solve nothing. Sit down, Fen, I'm not going to hurt you."

Fen swerved away from the dash he had been about to make as soon as they were on the terrace and did as he was told. They faced each other across the same table where half an hour before Giovanna had sat brooding on the sorrow of extinction.

"What did you think you would do with that stuff?" Giovanna asked, and answered herself. "Take it back to Chela and make some animals. Am I right?"

Thinking he saw a loophole of sorts, Fen began to explain how much he loved the animals he had come to know and how hard it would be to leave them behind, but the zoologist shook her head. "Your scheme was desperate, crazy, and doomed," she said. "Now tell me the truth and swear it by that amulet. Swear it on the tooth of the mir-akona, Fen. Where are the animals of Chela, that you must steal animals from Earth?"

Fen straightened, and she thought he grew a little taller as he stared not at her, but out into the stars, as if seeking his unimaginably distant home. Even his voice seemed to come from far away, from the cold void of interstellar space. "The animals of Chela are extinct," Fen said. "They have been dead at least five hundred of your years, but we mourn their passing as if it were yesterday. We Chelans murdered our animals—our birds, our mammals, our reptiles and amphibians, even our fish. We are left with nothing but insects and rodent scavengers."

Giovanna went numb with horror, yet at the same time wondered how she could have missed this terribly obvious answer to all Fen's mystery. Because it was unthinkable, she answered herself, and buried her face in her hands.

After a long time she looked up. "I can't take it in," she said.

He nodded. "I think you would have to grow up with it. For us it is history, as well as present grief."

"But how?"

His faint smile was not reassuring, and it occurred to Giovanna that she had never seen this pleasant being look cynical before. "Many methods were employed," he said, "most of them quite similar to the practices of twentieth-century Terrans. You were lucky, and we were not. Both planets whirled inside the lip of the vortex, but only Chela went down into the abyss."

Giovanna's head felt as if it might split, and she held it tightly with both hands. "No higher animals," she repeated. "All gone—the mir-akona and all the rest we kept asking about."

"I am sorry," Fen said. "Perhaps now you can understand that the subject is taboo."

"And you young people," she went on, "you so-called exchange students; let me guess. You are the fanatics, the seekers, who went out across the universe in search of animals and thought to repopulate your planet with a little suitcase of DNA."

"It was only meant to be a start," Fen cried. "We have been ordered to return. Ten days from now we must be at the spaceport, and we faced the prospect of going home empty-handed, without even a pet. Our mentor and friend, U-Bandor, is a great biologist who has searched all of his long life for an answer to the tragedy of the animals. We thought at least we could take him this."

"Would he have known what to do with it?"

"One of us has made himself an expert in the field."

"*Jesu Maria.* Did it never occur to you to ask for help?"

"No," Fen said. "It never did. It doesn't now." And before she could stop him, he rose from his chair and stalked away into the dark.

The container sat where he had left it on the ground almost at Giovanna's feet. She stared at it, poured some wine, drank a glass without tasting it, and stared some more. "Didn't eat any cookies," she mumbled. "Probably crash somewhere. Wish I could do the same." Instead she carried the container back inside, where she put on gloves and opened it. The little vials were in trays—twenty to a tray, ten deep—two hundred species if all the niches had been filled, neatly labeled ahead of time with their common names in English, a minor oddity that Giovanna filed away to think about later. "Alligator," she read, "fishing eagle, carp, clouded leopard, Thomson's gazelle, binturong, great white egret, herring gull, herring, fruit bat, dolphin, fennec fox, dwarf mongoose, yellow-billed hornbill, Blanding's turtle, reticulated python, Przewalski's horse." This stopped her for a minute until she remembered that this rare animal was the only member of the equine family stored at the Ark. For some reason Fen needed a horse and wasn't fussy about what kind. Giovanna read all the labels twice, closed the container, and set the dials to restore its diabolically cold temperature. She wasn't sure why she did this, but it seemed the right thing to do. Never had two hundred seemed to be so small a number.

Daria was awakened an hour before dawn by the ringing of the telephone, and suddenly there was Giovanna, tall and haggard on the screen at the end of the loft bed. Something terrible has happened, Daria thought. My tamarins are dead, or there's been a fire at the Ark.

"Forgive me," Giovanna said abruptly, "but this is news that could not wait, since it concerns Fen. He should be with you soon and must be treated with both compassion and perhaps a certain wariness. Let me try to explain."

Shivering in the tropical air of the August night, Daria pulled the sheet around her shoulders and tried to comprehend. When Giovanna finished speaking, they stared at each other in silence. At last Daria said, "I almost guessed. I kept saying to myself, it's as if there were no animals, and he was making it all up. But that was impossible, right?"

"Unthinkable," Giovanna said. "Yes. It was the same with me. I don't know what else to say. You must deal with Fen as you think best, and I must leave you to it. This event has raised issues I can't even begin to contemplate, and yet I must. *Coraggio, cara.* If you need me, I probably won't be here."

Daria watched the screen go blank and sat listening to the many small sounds that animals make in the dark. Outside the aviary dome a waning moon hung above the trees in a sky that would soon be flushed with dawn.

Knowing there would be no more sleep that night, she slipped into a tunic and went out into the moonlit garden and down the path to the pond. Here and there she could see the soft forms of water birds with their heads tucked under their wings, while overhead the bats swooped after their tiny, invisible prey.

It was on the promontory where they had had their first, strange conversation about animals that she discovered Fen and Peru. Fen was asleep, and Peru, who was lying down, had clearly consented to be his bed. The tall alien had his arm around the llama's neck and his face buried in Peru's withers. Most of the rest of him was stretched out on a mattress of heavy stomach wool. Peru gazed into the distance with a look both patient and pained. It was a scene that would have made Daria laugh an hour ago. Now, instead, she began to cry.

Fond as he was of Fen, Peru's feeling for Daria was of quite a different order. He had come to her as a little, bleating calf, and she had taught him everything he knew. Now she was in distress. Ever the gentleman, Peru was careful as he wriggled free, but Fen still ended up on the ground, looking dazed and bewildered. "Oh, Peru, you shouldn't have," Daria said, as the llama nuzzled her hair. "Poor Fen. He was so sound asleep, and then his bed got up and walked away." She gave a little, choked laugh that promptly turned again to sobs.

Fen rubbed his eyes and produced a smile of remarkable

sweetness. "That's all right. Peru must have thought you needed him more than I did."

"He can never stand to see me cry."

"I'm not crazy about it either," Fen said. "Please stop."

"I'll try," Daria said, wiping her eyes on the hem of her tunic, "but I just talked to Giovanna. Oh, Fen, why didn't you tell me? I would have understood. We could have done things differently and better."

"Nothing could have been better, Daria, and you must understand that the mass extinctions of Chela are a subject that most Chelans will not even talk about among themselves."

"That seems impossible to me," Daria said.

"No, it is merely peculiar from your point of view, and even I can see that it is a little odd. In Chelan history as it is taught, everything up to the beginning of the extinctions is ancient history, and that period is regarded as primitive and brutally ignorant. Then there is a gap of several hundred years and we have the beginning of modern, enlightened times."

Daria sniffed. "You're teasing me."

"Not at all, I assure you."

"Then how do you know..." Daria's voice trailed off, and she started again. "I mean, what you told me—it was vague, but there was an awful lot of it. Did you make it all up?"

Fen got up abruptly and walked down to the pond, where he stood, almost invisible, silvery grey in the dying light of the old moon. "It is hard for me to speak of this," he said at last, "but now I think I must and even want to." Slowly he came back and sat beside her on the ground, wrapping his long arms around his knees and gazing out over the quiet pond.

"I made some of it up," Fen said, "but not the important things. I didn't mean to suggest that those terrible years of Chelan history were really lost. They are quite well documented, and some Chelans, notably the group to which I belong, make an annual ritual of viewing the old films and photographs so that the memory of our animals will never die."

Daria felt a shiver go up her spine. "Films," she whispered. "You have films of your animals."

"Of course," Fen said. "It was a technologically advanced society. Without technology, I should think, it would be quite difficult to kill a whole planet full of living things. Hunting on that scale is just not possible for preindustrial beings. No, we have excellent films. It is just that no one wants to see them. I can't say that we want to see them either. We force ourselves to watch as the primate mother is slaughtered and her baby made into a hunter's plaything. We see the beaches buried in millions of poisoned fish, the forest animals starving among the fallen trees, the swift runners of the plains mounded against the fences that stood between them and the water they migrated hundreds of miles to find. Every year we sit down together very close to each other so that we can hold hands from time to time. Our mentors seem to have an inexhaustible supply of these pictures for our education."

"And then suddenly there was another world," Daria said softly, "a world that was brimming with animals. How wonderful."

"We really came without a plan," Fen said. "Our brief, if we had one, was just to see what could be seen. But greed and acquisitiveness are universal failings. We saw and immediately wanted to possess. I don't suppose taking the DNA would have worked. I've studied an immense amount of ecology, and I know how complicated it is, but to go back without a single animal was too heartbreaking to be borne."

"Do you all have pets?" Daria asked. She was thinking of his face as he cradled the fox kit in his arms.

"Of course," Fen said. "It was inevitable. And one of us has a horse. Not that size matters. Taking any of them back, even if we provided them with mates, would be wrong."

Daria felt as if she was going to cry again. The thought of the nine young Chelans, who so short a time ago had discovered the zoological miracle of Earth, having to leave it all behind was more than she could bear. "I think they should all come here before you have to leave," she said suddenly, the idea springing full-blown into her head and uttered before she had a chance to think about it.

Fen stared at her and laughed. "Now who is crazy?" he said.

"It's not crazy," Daria cried. "It's a great idea. I mean, it doesn't solve anything, but at least all of you can see a lot of animals and touch them and smell them and hear them. Well, you know. And we can spend a day at the Ark, or more, depending on when they get here. Think about it, Fen."

He grinned. "Lily would leave home, and even your remarkable mom would have a major hostess fit. This is no way for me to thank your family for its hospitality."

"We can put air mattresses on the lawn," Daria went on, as if he hadn't spoken, "and they can eat from the food slots. It will be dead easy and loads of fun. I'll stay home from school. Everybody can help with the chores."

"I think," Fen said, "that I need to eat and then, perhaps, to sleep for a day or two."

"Eat by all means, but call your friends before you sleep."

"You know, Daria, you remind me of someone," Fen said as he headed unsteadily toward the kitchen.

# twenty-two

They sat in a circle on the lush meadow behind the elephant house. From a distance they might have been hard to see against the grass, so green were they from the wonders of the day. Daria was with them, as was Giovanna, who sat on the stump of a great white pine, one of the first to succumb to the change of climate seventy-five years ago, in 2019. In contrast to the exuberance of the nine Chelans, the Terran women looked decidedly the worse for wear, especially Giovanna, whose dark-circled eyes nevertheless flashed with excitement.

"This has been great fun," Giovanna said. "It was clever of Daria and Fen to bring you all here, and it saved me a lot of trouble. Have you enjoyed your day? Is there anything else I can show you before we settle down to work?"

"Work?" Idron said. "Dr. Ferrante, we would do anything

for you, but what work can we possibly perform in the short time remaining to us here?"

"I am childishly fond of surprises," Giovanna said. Fen's heart skipped a beat without his knowing why. He reached out to take Filya's hand, but she snatched it away and pointed a trembling finger at the back door of the elephant house, from which emerged the figure of an ancient Chelan, who came slowly toward them, probing the unfamiliar path with a cane.

"U-Bandor," Fen whispered. "U-Bandor has come to take us home."

Giovanna chuckled. "No, Fen. U-Bandor has not come to take you home. He has come to work with you and with me on a project started by a young Chelan with a small stolen container of DNA, a project that may take all of us many years to complete. Daria, see if you can find a chair in the elephant office for our guest."

"No, no, I will stand," the old Chelan cried. "If I sit, I might fall asleep, and I am far too excited to do that. Look at me. I am as green as my youngest student. Melinya, what a beautiful cockatoo. Do birds flock to you wherever you go?"

"It is Dr. Ferrante's cockatoo," Melinya said in a barely audible voice. "It followed me from her office this morning."

"Damn bird has a mind of its own," Giovanna said. "Please put these kids out of their misery, U-Bandor. I'm so tired I couldn't explain how to unwrap a candy bar."

"Whereas all I have done is to wrench a spacecraft from an utterly recalcitrant government and then travel across a few thousand light-years to address this gathering."

"A mere nothing," Giovanna said, "compared to contacting every biological and conservation society in the country, the Senate subcommittee on Chelan affairs, the space agency, and five private foundations all in the space of a week."

"Please, you two," said Fen, who was not particularly in awe of either of them.

The great biologist leaned forward on his cane and looked down upon the nine—his protégés, the carriers of a long and ardent dream. "I have told the authorities at home that you are to stay here for a time doing vital research," he said. "They are not pleased, but what can they do? Send a gunship?" U-Bandor grinned a wolfish grin and went on. "When Giovanna reached me through channels so intricate we cannot hope to comprehend them, I saw at once that the hope of our planet lay here on Earth. Because, you see, the project that you persuaded poor Fen to attempt was merely naive, premature, and hopelessly undersize. In principle it could well succeed, and its elaboration will be our task over the next months and years."

"He assumes that money will be no problem," Giovanna said, rather tartly. "One wonders if Chelan science is that different from our own."

"The money will flow from Chela," U-Bandor said, "once the restoration of animal life on our planet is seen to be a genuine possibility. Just because we are dreamers and fanatics does not mean that others do not share our longing. It is, I believe, the defining characteristic of our race."

"I think the defining characteristic of your race is disrespect," Giovanna said, but she was smiling as she watched the young Chelans, who, having at least grasped the idea that they would not have to go home, were rolling on the grass and hugging each other.

Fen was the first to recover a semblance of sobriety. He disentangled himself from Filya, who was the most delicious shade of rose violet he had ever seen, and voiced the question that should have been on all their minds. "But what, exactly, are we going to do?" he asked.

"Make a biosphere to begin with," U-Bandor said. "That's why Giovanna is so fussed about money. We must build a Chelan biosphere here on Earth and test with the greatest care all those Terran animals that are thought to be candidates for life on our planet. This will be a long project and an expensive one. But as I said, money from Chela should be no problem. If they balk, we'll take time out to make them an animal—preferably a large, fierce animal—by way of persuasion."

"Then what?" Daria asked. "Will we send a sort of Noah's Ark? It sounds like a lot of animals to shoot through space, even if there's some huge improvement in space travel in the meantime."

"Now comes the hard part," Giovanna said, and both scientists laughed. "We have known for ages that live animals can be made from the DNA of dead animals, and this, of course, is the slender thread to which these young people tied their dream. The repopulation of Chela can be accomplished only if we are able at last to turn this so far very limited and specialized technology into something resembling mass production. Then, once the Chelans know what they want, they can produce it there from material much smaller and more portable than the contents of an ark. This is the final phase, and it is *years* in the future, but neither of us sees the slightest reason why, with enough money and work, it can't be done." She turned to the Chelans. "It may even turn out that we can re-create some of your own lost species. Don't get your hopes up, but so much will be discovered in the course of this work that our wildest dreams may turn out to be pale shadows of future reality."

"And how will our planet ever repay its debt to Earth?" asked Tendron.

U-Bandor smiled. "Put less politely, the question goes, What's in it for them? The answer is an old one: pots and pots and pots of money to do what they have been longing to do and couldn't afford. Because here is another facet to this jewel of an idea: we don't care whether we fill a small primate niche with a capuchin or a squirrel monkey, do we? Chela could become a nursery for the recently extinct animals of Earth."

Daria gasped and looked at Giovanna, who smiled and nodded her head.

"And now," U-Bandor said, "this ancient Chelan, who, unlike some of you, has not yet learned to do without naps, must get some sleep. It is my understanding that a banquet is being prepared at the house of Daria and that this is an experience for which one must be wide-awake."

# twenty-three

"I underestimated my parents," Daria said, "and even my gormless siblings have outdone themselves." She was standing with Fen on the knoll at the end of the garden and looking out on a scene of bizarre festivity. In the soft twilight of the August evening, paper lanterns swung from the branches of the oak and cast their glow over a long table laden with many kinds of food. With a few exceptions, the diners ranged in color from deep rose to shocking pink.

Roger, still wearing an apron and rather sweaty from the barbecue fire that smoldered outside the kitchen door, sat at one end of the table with Giovanna, while at the other end Gloria, in silver lamé and Navajo turquoise, warmed U-Bandor with the splendor of her smile. Tim, in his self-appointed role of wine steward, passed bottles and pitchers from guest to guest, and even Lily drifted decoratively along the outskirts of the party without committing herself to sitting down.

"This is the happiest day of my life," Fen said. "Ouch!"

"You really should put Scrabble in her cage while you eat," Daria said.

"And have her miss this wonderful dinner?"

"If you don't mind her dining on you, be my guest."

"Daria," Fen said, "I have a possibly too big favor to ask, something that would make life perfect instead of almost so."

"Which is?" Daria thought she had never seen him look embarrassed before.

"Well, everyone is to be housed at the Ark, you know, but I wondered if just possibly..."

"What about Filya?"

"I will see Filya every day at work."

Daria laughed and took his hand. "Dear Fen," she said, "I would have missed you terribly. And now let's eat. I am absolutely starved."

As darkness fell, Giovanna slipped from her chair and took the path that led to the wild side of the pond. A quarter moon silvered the black water; an owl hooted from somewhere in the woods; and staring into the shadowy spaces between the trees, she thought she saw for an instant a lithe cat form and a poised, small head with black stripes running from eyes to mouth like a trail of tears.